YUME NO HON

YUME NO HON
THE BOOK OF DREAMS

CATHERYNNE M. VALENTE

PRIME BOOKS

Prime Books

www.prime-books.com

AUTHOR'S NOTE: The chapter headings are taken from the Japanese calendar of the Heian period, which are in turn adapted from the Chinese calendar, which is made up of 72 divisions.

The chapter "Rotted Weeds Metamorphose Into Fireflies" is in part adapted from the Enuma Elish, a Babylonian creation myth.

The world of dew
Is the world of dew
And yet, and yet—
　　—Issa

THE EAST WIND MELTS THE ICE

Put a truce to any thoughts of departure. I am she who glides through the sky when the snow is falling fast, the lady of frost and darkness. I am a ghost, which is not to say I ever lived. I am a memory, which is not to say I ever died. I begin at the moment the ice on the river begins to crack like bones of glass. I am a silence written on pulp-mash paper, in ink drawn from village-wells.

Inward is the only conceivable direction. All arrows point within. So too, this book, which faces *down* and *in*, along the sallow thread of my tongue, into darkness and out again.

If I were to tell you that I am an old woman-hermit, who lives on the side of a mountain I cannot name in the year of the ascension of Taira Kiyomori, this would be true. It would, of course, be as true to say I stood outside the Theban wall whose mud-bricks are the color of pages and asked riddles with lips of verdigris. It would be as true to say I drove six brown horses around the walls of a burning city, that I gathered my husband in fourteen pieces and knelt in delta-silted river reeds with my arms full of his flesh. It would be as true to say I invented the world last year, from coffee beans and plantain leaves mixed in my veins. We are a body of Contradiction, flesh-full and fleshless.

But perhaps I am just a mad old woman squatting in the wreckage of a pagoda halfway up the mountain, mending my sandals for the seventeenth time and scraping in my bean patch, waiting for the new green shoots to slide out of the earth like stars. Perhaps I am only she, Ayako of One-Name-Only, who each night brews a sour tea of dandelion roots and watches the stars slide out of the sky like bean-shoots. It is possible that I only dream her, her rags and thin hands, her snow-cold calves and breathing eyes. It is possible I have never been anything but her.

If I do not dream her, then these are *my* hands deep in the soil of the Mountain whose silence booms in her heart as though it were an empty hall. If I do not dream her, then the others are a mist on the wild goose's wing , the dream of my lion-haunches and terrible teeth.

I wish to be dreaming her, so that I may call these others true.

LARVAE BEGIN TO TWITCH IN THEIR COCOONS

(To be alone is to work at solitude. It is very difficult, a lifetime's work, like the building of a temple. The first years are the carving of steps from camphor wood and the bodies of infant cicadas. Desire is still present like a moth—he flits onto your hair, your thigh, your smallest toe. He sits so quietly, small and brown, intricate as leaves. And you are not truly alone, because he is there, slightly furry against your skin, breathing.

The next years are the erection of a great Gate, red as poppy-wine, with guardian statues of jasper and knuckled silver. Now you are learning, you have begun to fashion your solitude with skilled hands, to chisel away at all that is not loneliness, to dwell in seclusion as you would in moon-white larval flesh. Desire has gone, but Need remains, and you look down the path for the shape of any human at all. Soon you begin to dream that they come. Your joints have begun to fuse, to make an utterly separate beauty.

The interior hall comes next, in shadow and rough-cut incense. You had thought yourself a Master already, but in these years like flapping crows you begin to scream, and your screams become the temple bells of perfect bronze, and you clutch their silken ropes, caught in the great work. These are the maddened years, when you have only the strangling Self. You are a pre-suicidal mass. There is no release from it now, and you begin to sow seeds in a little garden, understanding for the first time that there are no endings for you.

After a bushel of winters tied with chewed leather, the roof is laid out, corners dipped in boiling gold, arcing up towards the sky, which has begun to speak to you. You have polished and cut and painted with hawk's blood the edifice of your solitude, and it shines so under the dead moon.

And you are the icon, the holy relic to be housed. Your bones have calcified into sanctity. You are the created thing, unfathomably apart, clothed in antlers and rain-spouts. There is nothing now but you and Alone, not even a body, which long ago hushed itself into the snow-storms. It is completed, your *magnum opus*. A fontanel has re-appeared at the crown of your head, pulsing gold and silver—you are an infant again in the arms of the empty air.)

I have been alone for a long time.

FISH SWIM UPSTREAM, BREAKING THE ICE WITH THEIR BACKS

The dream-pagoda has five floors. It is red like dripping wax and in my cloud-body I have not climbed to the top. I think I meant to, once, but the cycles of fat salmon spawning took my smooth limbs and left juniper twigs. I huddle, or she does, the dream-Ayako, on the first level, against a wall that was once lacquered green and blue.

I cannot tell if it *is* me curled on the damp earth. The gray spider perched on her dusty wall seems equally myself. I apologize, it is what happens when the loneliness is built up and frescoed in costly paints. Solitude becomes populated with a legion of selves, each laid on each like stacked frames of film, like pig's ears in the noontime market, or the floors of a pagoda that once was red. The original is lost, just one of a thousand thousand silvern copies, scattered upwind.

Laying over the dream-tower is the dream-wall. It is brown, glum-grained and jaundiced by a Sun which frowns under her straw hat. Dream-men pressed the earth together to build it, and now it is my Nest. In this copy, which is not Ayako but comes from her like a long braid which begins at her crown, I can feel the bristle of fur like a bronze brush on my thighs, the jut of morphine-wings on my back. It is the dream of the lion-haunches, which is familiar as a shoe.

A Boy comes to the dream-wall. He is smooth and brown as an almond tree, with wide-set eyes and a cruel mouth. His hips sing of palm-oiled pleasures and I like him in a moment, because his beauty touches me like a hand. My paws are deep-padded and hungry—I breathe his smell in sheaves, smell of cinnamon and burned bread. My belly yearns for him, knows he is meant for me, will swell inside me like a black apple. I am certain of him, of how he will feel inside me, how his sweat will taste.

But he is waiting for me, and I oblige, for the dream-body knows the thing for which it is intended. Riddles, and games, and adulation.

"What is my name?" I ask in a voice like the sound of the Mountain gnawing his knees. The Boy looks at me with a quixotic raise of his brows.

"That is not a very good riddle," he replies, and I let his voice slide through me like spiced honey. He is worried, now, for he must suspect that he cannot possibly guess the answer among the possible answers that spread out in his brain like a Euclidean plane.. When he attempts it, I can hear his tongue thicken in his mouth.

"You are named Truth, for only Truth can loose what is bound."

And it is a good answer, better than most can dredge from themselves, pulling their words up like wooden well-buckets. My belly exults.

"No, beautiful boy, dream-within-dream. I am called She. She who travels when the snow flies fast. She who devours with woolen teeth. She who asks. I am all possible shes. There is no other She born under any mockery of a

It is possible that I only dream of her, her rags and thin hands, her snow-cold calves and breathing eyes. It is possible I have never been anything but her.

moon. I am the she-Wolf, the she-Axe, the she-Belly. I am the destination of that which is He. I cannot be guessed, and I am never known."

And then the dream-boy was inside me, in my throat and in my lion's stomach, whose ulcerated walls pulse in time to the flooding of rivers. My teeth drank him, and I slept in the corpulent sun.

Woman rises out of no-woman, and Ayako stirs in her sleep.

RIVER OTTERS
SACRIFICE FISH

Metamorphosis. It is a long line of bellies, chained together flesh-wise, circling each other in a blood-black smear. The sparrows pick cold red berries from the mud, the hawks pluck the sparrows from the sky. The fish swallow grasshoppers, the otters gulp down the fish. The world eats and eats and eats, and stomach to stomach it embraces itself. Hawk is Berry, Otter is Grasshopper. Woman is Fish and Sparrow.

Ayako sees this as she watches the new sun tiptoe on the river. She understands it, for she, too, has a belly which longs to pull creatures into it. The I-that-is-Ayako knows that dream-bellies also connect, along a strange umbilicus of tamarind bark and snow-pea shells. In the half-shelter of our ruined pagoda, I can see the stars, the constellations rotating in their angular anatomy. Over my/our flaxseed hair the kimono-sleeve stars tumble like lost feathers. The river whispers arcane spells, thick-voiced and gurgling with pleasure at the face it holds in its ripples, which is mine. The dream-face, with eyes of new apples, for in dreams, all eyes are green. The River and the Mountain split me between them—they have a treaty which is re-negotiated regularly.

Codicils are added, addendums and appendices drawn up with rustling laughter. There is no time here—Thursday has been killed in his sleep. They can afford to wait.

It is a small dream, this. It follows the seasons and eats orange *kabocha* squash boiled with wild greens. And into the dream occasionally some black-eyed boy or girl comes, to bring me a sack of rice or a little box of tea. They come from the dream-village, which has not the gentility to know it is a dream, because they pity the old woman on the Mountain. And I long to ask them riddles they cannot answer, I long to hold them belly-to-belly. They go back down the Mountain with innocent feet, back to huts and *miso* and smoked fish.

Because in her body, I hardly speak at all any longer. The rusted brass hinges of my voice have gathered dust. I put my/our hands to the soil of the garden, and can feel the heat of growing things, meant to be soon inside my body. The Mountain marks me, knows I am meant to be in *his* belly, etching his shape against the sky-that-is-not, pinioning the woman, the cobbled personae, the dancing cranes and bobcats and lizards and singing monkeys and squirrels to the slivers of dreams pretending to be stones. He gathers his blue and green and white to consume me, he gathers the gray and the gold. His chortling streams and the meadows lie restful and sweet, as though the moon-goddess had smoothed an emerald taffeta dress over her slender knees. He is impassive and huge, he mocks and waits.

Inside her/me the dreams are burning, falling, raw as bark-stripped pine. There is no sound where they step, for it is possible they are not really there, that these shadows are not theirs, that she is not doubled and tripled, tumbling backwards through bodies like scalding water.

And some secret avalanche on the far side of the Mountain rumbles as he clears his diamond throat.

WILD GEESE GO NORTH

I dreamed cannon-winds shot through my belly; each strand of wind carried talons and curved beaks which tore my flesh. My navel was cut out like a coin, my mouth was filled with dead leaves. I dreamed that I was the first belly. I dreamed my flesh dark and star-sewn. My womb bore up under a five-clawed hand, slit down a scarlet meridian, and black daises grew from the skin of its depths.

I dreamed it was Mountain who passed all these canine winds into me. He put his slate-blue mouth to me and took a breath that serrated the edge of the world. I felt his caves erupt in me, his glaciers and his footholds. I dreamed it was River who held me still, gripped my forearms in his hands like otter's paws.

I dreamed that I cried out to Moon, but she had been eaten whole.

The winds were in me and marauding, the teeth of Mountain nursing at my womb, and he filled me with migrating birds, he filled me with blade-wings that carved pictographs on the inside of my bones, where I could not read them. I dreamed that Mountain shook with pleasure as he emptied all his stones into me, the boulders and the pebbles and the granite flanks, and the sharpest wind which blows at his peak.

When I was filled with stone until I was too heavy to whisper, and wind until I was a body of breath, I dreamed that Mountain and River tore me to pieces with their teeth. They put my throat and my breasts into the sky frothing with whitecap-stars, and my thighs into the glistening rice-fields. They put my arms into the sea that boiled with serpents, and my hands into the desert, palms downturned.

And between them they ate my womb on silver plates, and called it perfection, called it their precious-sweet, their horn-of-plenty, their best work. They sugared it with marrow and lapped with agate tongues.

I dreamed I was dead in them, I dreamed I was scattered over the rims of earth.

And I dreamed that when he had swallowed his last, and I was a spot of blood on his beard, Mountain began to laugh.

SEEDLINGS SPROUT

The I-Ayako is satisfied with the progress of the beans. They have not broken the scrim of soil yet, but she can hear them wriggling beneath, like butterflies. She is worried about the turnips. Next year she will have courage enough to ask the dream-villager for some wheat to plant. She looks now to the crocuses peeking up their candle-tips. They will not keep her alive, but they are so sweet on her little pink tongue.

The wind is still cold when it comes down from the Mountain after its prayers on the peak. She would like to say it is a kimono that she pulls around her thin body for warmth, but long ago it abandoned its pinks and yellows and seems now little more than a blank cloth flung upon her.

My/her mouth aches like a shut box. I want so to speak, to moisten my lips and make my own wind-ablutions, add my verses to the Mountain's long poem. I am afraid it is broken, its tumblers have shattered in the winter freeze.

Thus one evening I went to sit at the foot of gnarled old Juniper near my pagoda and told him my story, which sprouted from my throat like a plum-tree. I do not know the juniper's name, but he is a good listener, and the moon rustled his branches while I spoke in a cobwebbed voice.

"When I was a girl and had a fine brocade *obi* and soft sandals, I lived in the dream-village. (I suppose it is possible that this is only a vision like the others, but I am here, and so I must have come from a Place, and one place-tale is as good as another.)

I had seven brothers who were all very wise and brave and they protected the huts and the market and the temple. But then came terrible men with their bodies covered in leather and iron, who swung long swords against the wind which screamed as they bit into flesh. They killed everyone, even my poor mother with her hair like a spider's best web, and they burned the temple to the ground.

I hid under a wheelbarrow for three days, until they had gone and the dream-village smoked black. I was very afraid. I wandered among the ashes of the bodies and wept.

Near dawn on the seventh day after the men had left, a Sparrow came to me with a fat red berry in her mouth. She ruffled her fine brown feathers at me and spoke: "Go and see Mountain," she said, "he will be your village, your father and your mother and all your seven wise brothers." Her fluted voice drifted off and, dropping the berry at my feet, took flight eastwards, towards the craggy toes of the sacred Mountain.

And so I took what clothes I could, a leaky water-sack I could mend, and the fat red berry and I went up the Mountain, following the path of the Sparrow.

It was evening again when I found her, perched atop my pagoda, picking at the ruined paint with her little gold beak. I waited for her to speak again, eager for bird-magic, but she did not. I held the berry out to her in my small white hand and she caught it deftly as she flew back to the village, leaving me to the tower and the Mountain.

It was difficult for the first years, when I had no rice or

tea, but Mountain provided for me cherries and plums and chestnuts, almond milk and cold green apples. After a time, people returned to the dream-village and children began to come to me and bring me little presents. Since I am a ghost, they wish to appease me.

And so we sit together and watch the origami-clouds, our dream-village of Mountain, Tower, River, Juniper, and I."

PEACH BLOSSOMS OPEN

They are suddenly here, floating on the trees like a cloak of butterflies, a blush creeping through their white petals. Suddenly the pagoda has beautiful handmaids which shower it with pale silks. There is warmth hushing through the sky. I lie under the trees with their flower-veils drooping low and I dream that in the afternoon I can see the eyes of a dream-husband in the blossoms.

I lay dreaming on the long-haired grass, legs brown and smooth as a sand dune, arched at the knee at the same angle as the tip of the Mountain, as the line that divides the sun-stone from the moon-stone, the shadowed side from the light. My toes wound in the reeds, tiny emerald rings on the dream-darkened skin, set with the diamonds of milky toenails.

See what in what regalia my dreams clothe me! Violets brush the small of my back with lithe, sugary movements. The scald of blue above me like a velvet gown, cut low on the horizon of my breast, clasped with clouds at the shoulders. See how it covers me in veils and layers of silk, rustling against my now-royal thighs with secretive grace, how it moves against me and strokes the skin. And the gnarled intricacy of these roots of a mountain ash for my Crown, jeweled in sap and leaves yellow as papyrus. What sovereignty my dreams supply! I am clothed in sky and bough, crowned in arboreal splendor. I laugh softly, let the wind imbibe my voice, the tonality melt into nothing like the wax of a candle-clock.

Lying so I looked up into the wind-braided branches of the dream-tree, its skin brown as the paint-pigment, the pale green of leaves against profound cerulean, the pink shimmer of flowers glinting like voices. They gleamed in the molten light, bright as blood, bright as the Dog-Star in the deep-blue days of summer to come. And slowly I saw, in the interchange of colors, red, green, brown, blue, white, that two of the blossoms were not blossoms, that their shade was not rose but the familiar olive-gold of his eyes, the dream-husband, staring blankly down from the branch, become the season's first fruit, snagged on a splinter of rose-tinged wood. Heavy-lidded, still rimmed in the kohl I mixed with my own fingers in red clay pots until the tips became black as cat's claws. I tenderly darkened his eyes that past dream-morning when he broke into pieces. I ran my fingertip over the fringe of eyelashes, letting my lips brush the iris as I move from eye to eye.

And now I lie under those eyes, against a tree which may or may not be on Mountain's flank, on the banks of the reed-jeweled river. I watch dream-crocodiles warming their bellies in the sun, regarding their mates with a fond reptilian eye.

I dreamed I had no trail to follow, that he left no blood-path. The dream-husband, the dream-brother, left me to scramble after him and clutch his body to me like a penance. I wandered, merely wandered, like a caravan-woman, my hair tied up into a crimson veil to keep the smoke-black length off my back . I did not speak, except to the hawks which flew at my shoulders, and they were silent.

But I also dreamed that beside me ever walks she, the second, or perhaps third self who knows none of this. I wander in her like an echo.

THE SKYLARK SINGS

The sun pealed out a hundred bronze bells smattered blue by
a bleeding sky.

Standing in the sacred "I" of limbs caught to , of *alone* on
a mossy stone with the stars combing my hair. I have smelled
the sizzle of my curls. I have clawed and screamed but no
one would venture close enough, no one's arm ever length-
ened to cup this body like a grail, and the Mountain gobbled
my voice like krill.

They are pathetic, my solitude and my dreams, they are
sodden and grotesque, dripping their shame on the summit
path, the filigree branches, the gossiping reeds. The river
roses tangled in a smear of obscene red as the dawn spilled
like milk over the tops of austere trees.

It is Water-Carrying day, when the Ayako-body walks
down to the River and fills its shabby clay jars. The running
stream asks me wordless riddles, the lark punctuates his
versifications with small pipings. I kneel and my knees
creak—I sadly recall a time when they did not. The newest
sun of a thousand warms my back like a winter dress as I
lean into the chortling brook.

"Tell me a lesson about water, River," I murmur, for River

has always been my tutor, less stern than Mountain in his dreaming heights. And when River speaks, his voice is yellow and blue, the fringe on an emperor's sedan chair, rustling imperceptible gold into the wind:

When you put your white foot into me, I part for you. But when you drink, though it is cool and sweet, you part for me.

"River," I say, "tell me a lesson about earth." And when River speaks, his voice is green and gray, the mist sloughing down into the valley.

If you plant your meager bed, perhaps a bed-tree will grow, perhaps it will not. But in the ranks of beds and trees and planters, only Mountain abides.

"River," I whisper, so as not to disturb the harp-tongues of the lark-flock, "tell me a lesson about wind." And when River speaks, his voice is white and rose, the air stirring new blossoms.

When wind touches the water-birds, it turns them the thousand colors of snow. Yet it does not change you.

"River," and now I am almost asleep again, my lips scarcely move to make the words, "tell me a lesson about fire." And when River speaks, his voice is tinged with red, its edges flushed and hot.

Flame travels on strange feet. Its heart is never twice the same.

And down by the dream-river, among jars of mottled clay, I sleep and write these lessons with the others on the tablet of my wax-flesh.

EAGLEHAWKS METAMOR-
PHOSE INTO DOVES

There is a dream-sister. She is all red, even her nipples that cut open the flesh of the sea. When the sun rises over our islands, which lie like a beaded necklace on the green waves, she drinks the light in a goblet of vines. When she sleeps, she sleeps in the curve of my waist, which is also red.

I dream there is no loneliness, I dream that she drinks my sorrow up like the dawn. This is the fire-dream, and I know it, for my limbs burn. I recognize the necklace of orange wedges and crab's eyes I wear, I recognize the bird-bright throat of my sister.

It is the fire dream and I am going to die.

I dream that it is River once more who holds me down with his turquoise hands, and my sister's arms are full of stones. One by one she brings the black rocks down onto my body, my sky-skull, the fine bones of my flaming feet. My lava-blood spurts like semen from throttled skin, leaping out as if it hated me. She crushes me under her vitreous stones, under her talon-hands, under her grunts and screams like a skewered boar.

I am not afraid. My bones grind to dust with joy, frenzy,

the marrow liquefies ecstatically. In River's strange-nailed grip I writhe and laugh, tiny flame-hiccups erupting from my bloodied lips. She rains down on me white-eyed quartz, basalt, feldspar, granite. She stuffs my mouth with dream-coal like an apple, and I can feel the seraphic pleasure of my teeth cracking. She is releasing me, and my flesh gobbles her stones as greedily as a child.

The dust-stuff of my bones River gathers together and mashes with rice-paste and goat-fat; into this he pours plaster-of-paris. He makes of me an island chain, rounded as beads of sweat bubbling to the surface of the froth-torn sea.

And I rise out of my bones like steam—they are nothing but mute earth, now. I am a naked fire, with breasts of naphtha and sardonic knees, I am beyond what once was the red of flesh and the dream of the sister, the crab-iris of my pendant and the blue molars that River sunk into my neck so tenderly as the last rock rushed down and bit into my brain.

In the dream I am free, I range out, flitting from place to place, faceless, formless and wild, painting my scalded heels with ocean. The jellyfish pout in the harbor like little mouths, translucent and pure, swallowing nothing. All paths are taken—I fan out over possibles like hair on lightless water; my matchstick-braids swing wide and encompass heartless mountain-architectures, skulls and steppe-altars, the shape of a crone scraping circles into the sand.

I am a body of flame, without steel-jointed bones. The dream-sister released me and only the fire remains, the fire and the voice, my voice, that ever-owl-screeching voice, banshee-bright on a hundred infant hills which are the old body, which thump like a suffocating trout, tail to the starry south.

THE SWALLOWS RETURN

"Why do you not go up to the second floor of the pagoda?"

I leapt up from the rush-bed of River, the hair of Ayako-I tangled up with twists of milky grass. A great Mountain Goat stood before me on hooves of pyrite, his shaggy wool twisted gray and white, snow and stone, colors of the roots of old things. His horns were monstrous, swept back from his mossy brows in pearl and jaundiced bone.

"It is not so very far," his voice ground, like a stone moving aside to reveal a cave. It was not surprising that he should speak—when you have built your solitude-temple as I have, many things speak which should not.

"I cannot get to the top. My feet are weak and stupid, now. My knees are like paper boxes." The Goat seemed to shrug in his tangled skin, his black eyes shifting shades from jet to coal to the roof of a smoking temple.

"I did not say you ought to reach the top. But the second floor is not so great a feat. Why not unfold your knee-paper and climb? If there is a tower, there must be a climber, else why would the tower stand?" With this his hooves clattered on the stones and he was gone, up the side of the mountain where the wildflowers grow all dewy and bright.

Ayako is refuge. I am profound within her. She is the simplest of dreams, perhaps my best one. She trembles and is hungry for fish and rice, she fears storms and has silent flesh which rustles like a robe. I am afraid for us, that if the I-that-is-Ayako ascends the red tower, I will become lost in our/her dream-women, and I will not be able to tell the dream of the lion-haunches from the dream of the belly-winds.

But we had young turnips and mustard greens in our befuddled stomach that day, and these things make bravery.

So I-in-her stood in the center of the pagoda, in the cross-hatch of shadows and strewn stalks of sun-leeched grass, looking up through the ruined levels, rising and rising like angular suns. I found a foot hold in the wall, and a ledge to grip, and thus worked my way upwards. There had once been a fine painting on the pitted stone, I could still see shabby colors in the cracks—a bull's head, a burning horse, a woman giving birth beside a river.

I was a column of sweat by the time I pulled myself through the mildewed floorboards and into the second room.

In a corner long ago conquered by fierce and noble spiders lay a leather wine-sack, an intricate moon finely wrought upon its surface, and it was filled with goat's milk, which was sweet and warm.

THUNDER LETS LOOSE
HIS VOICE

When you come to the sun-wall, you expect a Question. A Riddle. But because you do not know, cannot know, which on is peculiarly yours, all Questions are asked. Only when my scarlet-dripping mouth opens around the divine interrogative does one Question gain ascendancy. Before I speak, all the Questions that ever were lie under the possible quiver of my leonine tongue. And so, because any Question may be there, soft as a eucharist, all Questions *are* there.

Equally, all these Questions are answered. (This is the logic-dream, intersecting the dream of the lion-haunches at consecutive right angles.) Before you speak, all answers jumble themselves behind your acoustic uvula, a traffic in conceivable responses, as though they fled from some dark monster for whom no answer exists. Before you speak, you could say anything, and so you have said everything.

Further, before you ever came to my dust-bricks and the slow slide of my paintbrush-tail, all the Questions and Answers have been uttered, rejected, accepted, stuttered over, well-orated, and guessed at. You have been eaten, regurgitated, defecated, decomposed. I have been slain, flayed, skinned, vivisected and displayed on your mantle for generations. You have killed the king and married the queen, blinded yourself and died in obscurity. I have picked my teeth with your metatarsals and sunned my belly on the grass. It has all *occurred*.

And yet, before any of them have occurred, it is possible that all have occurred, and so they all have. There is no reason for us ever to meet. We have already met. I am in your belly, you are in mine. We are a many-colored *ouroboros*, merrily chewing on each other's scales. My riddles are answered. I am content.

And yet you keep coming, to find in me the snarled yarns of a thousand and one imaginable universes of envowelation and verbiate gesture—words and words and words, a tower of possible vocabularies, a geography of lingual variation.

It is possible that women are like this, too. That from a single source they dilate into all possible women, like a flame changing colors from the center outwards in wide bands: white, blue, yellow, orange. It is possible that all women are one woman, who has already lived, died, conflagrated and drowned.

It is possible that men are also connected this way.

Despite this, I love because it is my nature the dream-taste of all possible flesh on all possible tongues.

THE FIRST
LIGHTNING FLASHES

The milk was warm and thick, better than the throat-that-is-Ayako has had in many years. In the early days I used to pray to Mountain to send me a little goat I could love and who would keep me warm with her wool, whom I could milk. Perhaps I could even strain cheese from the milk. Instead he sent rabbits and squirrels to eat. But I did not complain.

And strangely, with the sweet milk circling my teeth I was completely Ayako. I was within her tightly and hotly, blooded and fleshed. The dream-women fled and I was the white singularity at the center, open, iconic. Self flowed into self and all things flowed selfwards. The milk seeped through me in ornate patterns, a complicated knot work separating fractal-bright in my veins, which in themselves separated and separated further like winter branches thinning into twigs.

I was truly alone for a moment, and the temple was whole, gilt-edged. Incense sighed from my pores. I forgot the lion-dream and the fire-dream. I forgot the dream-husband and the dream-sister.

The phosphor-stars shone through a hole in the distant roof, and clouds drifted over the moon like mendicant's rags. And under their house-blankets and mist-curtains I was Ayako, and no other.

But soon the wine-sack was empty, and sleep brushed my ears with her ash-lips.

THE EMPRESS TREE FLOWERS

In my dream, I begin to plan a revenge. My breasts and my thighs conspire.

Mountain cuts an alpine range through my torso, tumescent summits swell up horribly, boils of dirty snow. River is rewarded for his complicity, he flows now directly into the mouth of my womb. I am his banks, I am his delta, I am his floodplain. His fat throat giggles as he encourages himself into frothing rapids along my cattail-ovaries.

But inside the dream of the belly-winds, the revenge-dream begins to form like a gilled fetus, in a *satori* of suspended animation, poised on a curious tiptoe like a Neolithic messenger-god. I am horribly open between them; they have polished my skin like banisters so that they can live inside me, playing checkers on my painfully elongated spine.

Quietly, I start to gather clouds across the black line of my collarbone, to hide the star-areolae from their sweating glances, from Mountain and River, who hold my battered legs open. I take the stars away, I rob their treasure house of all those white jewels, I let them laugh and drink from me like tavern-thieves and all the while I am robbing them of all possible skies.

I turn the dream-oceans dark, shade by shade. They deepen like a bruise: yellow, blue, indigo, black. I spit pigment into the waves, onto the new islands that have burst up in the west, onto the silent continents. I stain everything black. There are no harbors, there are no ports.

But there are villages. River coughs, Mountain smokes his pipe, and between the saliva and the smoke I find thatched roofs in my knee-pits, marketplaces in my sternum. They sink wells in my tear-ducts. I suckle a generation of water-diviners.

I hear them whispering, where a tributary winds up the cloud-side of Mountain. They are planning a Palace of my teeth. Molar-turrets, incisor-halls, portcullis of canines. When it is finished it will block my throat and I will never speak again. They send in canaries and cartographers to map the veins of usable enamel.

But they work slowly. I have time.

MOLES METAMORPHOSE
INTO QUAILS

A hawk sat that evening in the pink flush of sunset picking at grass seeds, not looking up or down, only at the seeds which will now never sprout. And possibly I, too, the Ayako-body and the fire-body and the wind-body and the lion-body and the wife-body, germinate together in some dread aviary stomach wall, fed only by blood and bile and the occasional field mouse, growing dark and strange, with limbs the color of pupils. In the mirror of gastronomy I do not recognize a woman, only flesh, only bone, only the swift-scarlet ventricles of quickening tongues. I see only multiplicities. My feet are rooted in this unimaginable belly, as are theirs. Toes disappear into fluid, into soft veins and pulsation, into rhythms inconceivable, irredeemable, and un-patterned. In the belly of the hawk I am silent, in her thick body I am still.

I climbed down from the tower—down is always easier than up. When in doubt, head downward. By the time my joints have accomplished it, a weak moon has drifted out of the black like an afterthought. I made my small cooking fire on the familiar earth near the crumbling *torii* gate and boiled a thin stew of bamboo shoots and young potatoes.

It is all the same to me whether her hair is the color of a burned oak or of the fire that burned it. But like all my postulants, she is beautiful. She smells of alfalfa and licorice.

After a time, the Gate seemed to loom larger and I spoke to it, my second tutor, whose architect was ash, a body that had long ago burned out like a cigar.

"Gate," I said, "tell me a lesson about cooking-pots." Gate did not turn towards me, but her voice was thick, paper-pulp fashioned into a mouth.

They evolve like drawbridges, they open and shut.

"Gate," I mused, "tell me a lesson about tea-cups." Her voice ran like paint, trickling down her red flanks.

They are the nature of empty, there is nothing in them but that you put it there.

"Gate," I bowed this time, for Gate is much gentler than River, "tell me a lesson about chopsticks." Her words stood still and vibrated.

Enough of them together line a passage down to the belly-throat, where all things occur.

"Gate," I whispered, "tell me a lesson about hunting-knives." Her voice fell on me like a shiver of pine needles.

They are origin.

Hot stew simmering contentedly in me, I curled against her once-beautiful wood and the constellation of the sea serpent coiled overhead.

THE FIRST RAINBOW APPEARS

She is my dream-self, my night-self, she is my deep-self, she is my obverse, my androgyne-self despite her full lips and curving limbs, my hunter-self, my archer-self, my earth-self. The self-that-is-wife. She is the god-self that must rest within like a child when I eat beneath the Gate. She is embodied and unbodied, the Saturnine sliver of me that haunts the corners of my elbows, eyelids, and sits fecund in her smoke-lodge creating universes from pine needles. That swallows the world whole like a golden-bellied snake and excretes mythos like sweat from her crystal-scaled skin. The dream-body walks the desert on feet cut by thorns, with scratches on her palms and date-juice on her lips. She is made of earth. But within me walks the unscathed and unmarked, and she is made of light.

I dream I have smashed clocks and pocket watches and sundials and bronze-orbed pendulums to feathered-glass razors, pulverized their round faces into metallic dust. I dream lilies grow from the inner curve of my skull. I dream I can see the muscles in my/her back slide and move beneath her foxglove skin as I moves beyond it, into the next self that dissolves into seafog when I strive to see the one after, to see myself in her body, sheathed in her hair, to unite with her, to be a whole. I walk in the brittle sun and she waltzes under the arctic blaze of the north star.

I/she found your jaw today. It cast a shadow, delicate and wavering on the water, the shudder of a waxwing shaking rain from her feathers. The shadow eclipsed the water, and the water eclipsed the stones, stealing glimmer from the stream and silt. Deep in its fingers lay a row of perfect moon-teeth embedded in pink flesh and a ridge of perfect bone, torn and bloody as a trout in the jaws of a hawk.

This is the dream of the sister-wife, and in it the silt-body becomes a narcotic, a morphine that encourages nothing but forward movement, denies the lateral progression of these beggared forms. She is sheer color, needle-wings of every irised shade. In her morphine river I drift like a raft of yellowed reeds.

FLOATING WEEDS APPEAR

I have used the last of my tea. The dream-village boy brought it last summer folded into a square of yellow cloth, holding out the wrinkled green leaves to the Ayako-I with trembling hands. He was in awe, to see a living ghost, with her flesh looped over bones like knitted shawls, and hair that brushed the back of her heels like a kiss. His eyes were so wide, offering his tea as though I/we were a statue, a wood-woman covered in gold leaf, worthy only of terror and service. I imagine they draw straws for it, the honor, or shame, of bringing me these small gifts.

But I have used the last of it, and I must wait until summer to drink my tea again under the slow-blink of starlight. Perhaps it is just as well—my teacups, rough hewn from River's fleshy clay, do not stand up quite right. Some of the tea is always lost, the sour green liquid sits at an awkward angle and sloughs out when my fingers brush the rim. My fingers, my dream of fingers, are not so graceful. I lose the tea, down my chin, out to glass, onto the earth. I cannot keep it all in my mouth. I am too small for it, and the cups too poorly made.

The wine-sack, too, is gone. I woke, forcing the Ayako-eyelids open as early spring sunlight pried at me greedily, and it was gone. I think perhaps it is wrong for me to miss it. I think I should be content with what Mountain brings and ask for nothing else. Then again, perhaps it is not me.

I warm water in my little pot and pretend I can taste the sharp star-points of tea in my throat. It is enough, but somehow, it is not.

DOVES SPREAD THEIR WINGS

I stand in my cloak of embers and stir the dream-earth, my skin-scald medieval and slant-eyed. Sage, peppermint, wormwood are scorched beneath me—I care nothing, nothing at all. Rain like inkwells pummel my sternum, my haunch. Away from the islands that River made, the ion-trail that is my flesh sears the sky.

There is nothing here but the fire-dream, the savage flesh and the stern destroyer, nothing but death under the wide elms, the staunch oaks, death under my own eyes bleeding gold paint, my frescoed mouth, flooded with tempura and cobalt-poisoned blood, the lead of murder-pipes.

I choke, I cough up a wreck of wood pulp and iodine, I drown in my own fluid-flame, in the churned death of volcanic paths, the whirling leaf-self which dervish-scours all in me that would lie well in beds of birch-bark, in beds like paper, where books like this one, which is not mine but *hers*—the dream-hermit, where books like hers are written in sweat, the manuscript of elongated muscles illuminated in diamond salivations.

I am a vessel of salted meat, eyes glazed over by an abundance of nights, a surfeit of dream-visions wherein I touch human breath. There is a film over my dream-body, a veil which cannot be touched or torn. My heart beats seven times and stops, ventricles covered in thick gasoline. It is only in the stopped heart, the deadened pulse that I can discover any revelation, that any ease is to be unearthed.

I am already blackening the soil, already devouring the root systems of baobabs and dandelions, already seething in my half-living skin. Stamp, stamp, stamp, beast rampant on a verdant field and I am nothing but a heraldic smear, blood on stained glass—the sun refracts through me onto the faces of the faithful and I am again only skin, only surface, only the fur and lip of a woman.

Seize this chimeric body, this betraying flesh and it will always and only escape.

I am a tooth, a body of teeth, and I pierce through as though the world were made of water. What else can I ever be but this black-eyed eater of men? What patchwork breasts can I offer up to the screaming stars that will ever satisfy their dark tongues? My back flares wide and strong under the sky, under the moon with horns like mine. Alone I corrode the earth, alone I carve shapes into the path. I walk uncloven, and open my woman's mouth to swallow darkness until my jaws crack.

I search for a city, I search for walls. I search for the dream of flammable materials.

THE HOOPOE DESCENDS
TO THE MULBERRY

The boy who brought tea had clean fingernails. That is how I knew he was a dream—what villager can keep his hands clean after working in the rice fields, at the butcher, the blacksmith, mending the well-rope, spreading pitch on the bottoms of fishing boats? So I spoke to him, since dreams are my peculiar surrogate family, I felt I had the right. That it was my duty to address the dream and call it by name, so that it would stay and join all my other dreams in their agate-toed walk. After all, I had no boy-dreams.

He was very pretty, with unkempt hair and limpid eyes. His narrow hips seemed to jut a challenge, though I am long since the days when the hips of men pointed to me. He extended his offerings to me, trembling—he was the fear-dream, then, the dream of cold sweat. I liked watching his hand shake, as though I could curse his line with a glance and a muttered phrase. I liked the quiver of his brown skin.

A sack of rice, a woolen blanket, and the beautiful-smelling tea leaves, which sat in their yellow cloth like oblong jewels. I could see the whites of his eyes, terror-moons lodged in his skull. I readied myself for the great effort of speaking with the throat-and-belly instead of the mind-and-heart. It is altogether a different skill.

"Boy," I said, and I was ashamed of my broken voice, creaking like a brass hinge, "tell me a lesson about the village." I waited eagerly for the dream to speak. I loved my lessons, I was eager for more than River would give.

But the boy only gurgled in his throat, an animal, horrified noise, and with a yelp threw down his bundle and ran back down the Mountain path. Behind him a dust-cloud rose up like an eyelid, and closed again.

Ghosts are not supposed to speak. It is considered impolite. And now I must wait a full year to try and catch the villager-dream again.

SPARROWS SING

I flex my gold-shag paw under a drumskin-moon. It is easier here, in the lion-dream. All that there is on the Mountain is solitude, each of whose notes must be plucked on the harp-strings at just the right time so that the music of my disintegrating self will arc over this land like a temple ceiling, and with as many colors. That is not concerned with me, with asking and answering. In considering the whole, one possible woman is not enough. Only in groups, in clusters like cattle-stars, can they bee seen for what they are.

I ought to remember the name-riddle. It is a good one. The boy who called me Truth still swims within, a seven-gabled fish. Between Questions there is not much to do but lie on the wall, devouring grape-pulp and mashed cardamom, resting the muscles in my back. I have a peculiar anatomy, being a winged quadruped, and the weight of wings on my thick-knobbled spine gives me pains. The city doctors will not come—and who can blame them? If I asked them which roots and roasted leaves would be a salve to me, their saliva would dry in their mouths. If they answered incorrectly I would be within my rights to swallow them whole. It is the nature of things: any Question I utter must be answered with blood—mine or theirs.

This is the dream of science. In this feline body I am bound to examine myself, as though I were a butterfly skewered on a wax board. *Maculinea arion.* Save that I am also the slim silver pin and the thick wax and the hand that affixed these things. When I look at my flesh it looks back.

This is the dream of separateness. I am not the city I guard. They fear my scythe-claws no less than my mausoleum-tongue. I am sub-urban. The hermit-dream lies with her boiling visions somewhere higher than her city, a superior altitude that forgives her this geography of the unreal. I am beneath and outside my city, I circumscribe it, I keep out the unworthy. We are on the outer edge, beyond the pierce-reach of copper compasses.

Momentarily, I am the men I eat.

But that passes.

EARTHWORMS COME OUT

I have become accustomed to the second floor of the dream-pagoda. A few centipedes, with bodies of jointed rubies, have made my acquaintance. The floorboards have fallen through in places. Dust and flecks of paint hang suspended in the air which is often gold these days, under a haze of low clouds that suggest the sun.

Ayako moves more slowly now, as though she/I cannot connect to her body. I hope that when the dream of the villager comes again I will be able to catch him—I think another dream might cure the creaking of her bones. I hate the sound. The other women do not creak.

Everything is full but this body—the rains have brought worms wriggling into the mud, and River's fat pink fish are full of the worms I have dropped into their throats. The trees are made of flashing wings. My little garden teems with thick young shoots, pale green and dark, promising that I will not starve come winter. But the body is empty. I hardly live in it at all these days. The sun makes it lazy and I drift into the dream-women with diagonal ease.

A gentlemanly brown Moth flits in and out of the pagoda. He wears his creams and fawns with the grace of a salaried courtier. He sits in the shadows and lets his antennae waft with the breeze. Often he will land on my hair or my sandals, (which require mending again) and his furry belly will rub imperceptibly against my skin.

"Moth, tell me . . . " I whisper in a voice like an autumn frog-song.

"Yes?" he hisses, rubbing his paper crane-wings together.

"Nothing."

CUCUMBERS FLOURISH

This morning, before the dream-sun could report me, I swallowed one of their villages.

I simply drew my knees together and it vanished, caught between my moss-bones and my vine-skin. I felt the roofs splinter and pop against me, the cattle scream and the temple bells shatter. My thighs exulted, trembling with a shivered joy. I tried to conceal my sighs of delight as they all crushed inwards and were finally silent.

When my knees fell back, there was no trace. Mountain and River did not notice. They are busy with the Palace. They have called the ocean creatures together to fill a great jade vat of ink, in order to inscribe their names over the Gate, and the History of the World. River rests the vat on my belly while he blows smoke rings at the scaffolding which has by now obscured my jaw almost entirely.

I am wasting. I begin to wonder if the villages would sustain me. If I only swallow a few at a time, perhaps they will not notice. They have set the red sun on my steps, and he is now my gold-chinned jailor, arcing over me, back and forth, dragging his great clunking cloud-chains behind him.

There is much activity on my body, and they have poured

the foundation of the Palace from a blood-mash of cartilage. The miners tap, tap, tap at my jaw through the night, piling up teeth like cairns, piling them up in wheelbarrows and crates, in baskets and slings. I have heard Mountain suggest seventeen balconies. River plans a tower from which to view the History, when it is finished.

THE BITTER HERB
GROWS TALL

I must confess that there is another dream. It is the dream of
the silent girl. It is very small, and the I-that-is-Ayako is
ashamed. It is not nearly so grand as the others.

In the dream I am wearing gray—very soft, cat-like. I
am washed in blue light. The dream-girl is alone, for all
of the dream-us is alone. We come from Ayako—we
cannot be other than she, and she is alone beyond dreams
of solitude.

Her dream-hair is drawn into a knot at her neck, but
strands have escaped and blow darkly against her shoulders. This dream does not move. She does not change. The
heart in her beats very slowly, and she wets her lips from
time to time. After a pass of her delicate tongue, the lower
lips shines silver. That is all.

She peers out a window at a long expanse of trees, which
whisper to each other in the night, passing along what
rumors there are that concern trees. In front of her/me is
well-made paper, stacked together neatly, as if we meant it
to stay; all her pens lie motionless in their pots. She has rings
on her knuckles, and she taps them against the paper,

making a thickly muffled noise. But other than this she does not move, and the paper is blank.

I do not know why she sits at the bottom of the Ayako-belly like a solemn stone. But she is there, and in their orbits, the dreams seem to turn towards her as they pass.

GRASSES WITHER

I found your clavicle, white as a wand. The grasses are beginning to turn brown at the tips now—not much, but a little, the gold before rot sets in. In the dream of the sister-wife, they seem to wave like tiny hands, the hands of children drowning. It called out to me among the reeds, plaintive and small.

I dreamed that I wanted it, the long chalky expanse, lying in the red soil like a hyphen—the sentence of your body unfinished. I wanted to put my mouth to the ulcerated predicate, to complete you with my tongue and lips and teeth, to bite you off and continue the flesh of you down into my own. In my hand it looks alien, an infinitive from a foreign language covered in bone.

I dream that I hate the owner of the bone. The dream-brother, ghost-husband. I collect him like marbles over half a desert, I crouch in the silt-ridden delta until I have sunk to my knees, grub his filthy bones and chunks of flesh from the earth, to pile them together in a grotesque cairn. When I found his intestines I had to loop them over my arms and around my neck, where they hung slimy and stinking, a mottled serpent-noose. They tried to drag me under.

It is what I was made for. The dream-search and the spill of his organs like egg yolks on glass. I hate the smell of him now, the curdled scent of his veins turned inside-out. It is all over me, gesticulating in my pores, his foreign sweat.

Yet I want the clavicle. It is smooth and clean of flesh. Dreaming within my dream I put it to my lips and play his collarbone like a macabre flute. My cedar-dusted fingers press into the marrow and low notes exude, sibilant and lurching down its barometric octave. Music throttles itself and serrates the wind.

Wherever the sound touches, the grass separates into dust and falls to the starving earth like a handful of torn pages.

I dream that he is death in death.

BARLEY RIPENS

I-Ayako has become ill. I watch her retch by the River with disdain. Her body heaves like a blown sail when the wind changes. I hate that she is old, that her skin is no longer beautiful. Below, in the valley of the dream-village, shocks of green writhe like demoniac oceans—the barley comes of age and the I-Ayako adds our body's sloughing to the earth.

My hands are not mine. Fingernails half-grown, jutting out like moons buried in a black-soiled field. I am only this lurching body. I am only this. These.

Yet, I begin to wonder about the body which hangs on me like torn clothes. If she dies, what will happen to us? Is there an I-above-all? An ideogram that is me and I and Ayako and all the dreams together—is there a divinity of first person? A prime mover of our limbs? We are afraid that she is failing us, that she will keep lurching into the water, vomiting and vomiting until she empties herself completely and we too have gone out of her by the throat-road. We are afraid the cramping body is the only real.

If she dies, will we simply blow apart, pine needles in a swift wind? Do the dreams possess location? Are we locative, dative, ablative? Where is the language of Us?

I crouch in the silt-ridden delta until I have sunk to my knees, grub his filthy bones and chunks of flesh from the earth, to pile them together in a grotesque cairn.

What linguistic calculation could be made which would result in our variable, our presence outside of the Ayako-equation? We are cross-multiplied, we are exponential. She is not.

I am Ayako, and since she cannot answer, I cannot. When she/I drink our tea-less water, it falls into the flesh with worry edging its taste.

But in the morning it had passed, and our belly was calm.

MANTIDƧ ĦATCĦ OUT

I dreamed of a great maze. It turned underneath me, left and right and over itself, a great snarl of brick and mortar. It was painted and at each turn a color faded into its mate, so that the whole expanse curled like some impossibly complex sea serpent—perhaps if I had lingered I could have read some forbidden language in its knot-work. I could almost scry its subterranean tongues, reaching into the earth—down, down, down.

It had a physiology, a throbbing anatomy of stone and pigment. I could mark the pathway of its blood, through arterial thoroughfares and bile ducts, descending organs, kidneys, tangled intestines. It was a body, whole and complete, but one which contained the bodies of others like stacked dolls—strange-skinned creatures with blank eyes, and in the shadows a great black bull tossing his horns. I dream it lies below me, its skin touching my skin, like a prone lover.

I put my dream-lips, my flaming mouth to it. But I am a virgin, I have not done it before, so of course, the fire spreads too quickly. It blanches the twisting walls, blackens the creatures to skeletons, doors to molten piles of knob and hinge. I arch my back and my breasts brush the bull-horns and the great wooden gate—they shatter into pyres. My toes curl at its angular walls, my incandescent womb opens and shuts, clamping at its architecture, clutching wildly at the maze. I am a holocaust, breathing heavily and writhing over my adored labyrinth, twisting my legs around its girth. I am the inferno, clamping my body over the adulated—and who could find the blood of my virginity in the embers of this city?

Everything is red now and I dream my own laughter is a scorch-mark, my thighs tightening on the maze-roads send them up like cheap matches. My belly lifts up and a rain of naphtha-sweat gleams on the already engorged flames—and I am laughing, laughing, laughing as I burn divinity into this place.

What could I ever be but this black-eyed eater of cities?

When I leave the dream maze, still full of my heat and sweat, I can smell the flesh of the bull cooking, smoky and sweet.

And I search again, for another, for the beloved, for the bed-notch, for a city who will sing my love out in unmeasured lyrics.

THE SHRIKE CALLS

"What did you want to ask me that day?" the Moth mused in his thick voice, rubbing his forelegs together lazily. I sat with him in the shade of the second floor, escaping the early summer heat.

"I was going to ask you for a lesson," I answered. "Gate and River tutor me. More often when I was young, but still, from time to time."

"I am only a Moth, I know how to eat wool and seek light. If you want to know these things, I can teach you."

"No. I am not sure there are answers which would have meaning for me any longer. I am a bad student. I am too weak to be the wife of Alone."

The Moth shrugged. "Why do you not go up to the third level? Perhaps there is something there which would have meaning for you."

I-Ayako looked up through the slatted floorboards, the slant of unassuming light that filtered through to land, moth-like, on my open palm.

"It is so far. I have only just come to this level."

"I do not wish to stay in your pagoda. I have heard rumor of a beautiful flame in the city, and I go tonight to meet my family there. So I cannot tutor you. I do not have the time. Ask the third floor." And with that, the Moth spread his stately, cream-spattered wings and flitted out of the tower.

It was a far more difficult climb than it had been to the second floor. The walls were smoother and bore less paint. I tore three fingernails in the ascent, and when I pulled myself, almost weeping, onto the next knotted floorboards, my hands bled freely.

The angled room was bare except for a few forlorn grasshoppers and a small statue which stood in the far corner. Time had erased its face from the stone, but it stood, calm, seraphic. Gray featureless rock stared out at me and there were no sounds save the cries of prey-birds circling.

THE BUTCHERBIRD IS SILENT

I dream that I can string the Questions and Answers together on a long line of catgut, like little wooden prayer beads, or a thread drawn through thick leather. I dream I can see them all around my shaggy neck, sparkling against my fur. I hold the heft of them in my paws, matched pairs like chromosomes, *AB, CD, KL, XY.*

I hold a plethora of halves. Each time a man comes to gain entrance to the city, he completes a set and my collection grows. It is an art, and I am skilled at it. Perhaps at the end of time I will truly hold them together like a great necklace, a grand unified theory of interrogation. Each time their flesh touches my tongue with dark and secret flavors, I inch closer, my books tilt towards balance.

A boy came wandering with heavy-lidded eyes, the droop of the lashes that can only mean extreme enlightenment—or opium addiction. His fingers were long and pale, funereal, with fingernails I imagined would taste of ripe dates. I began to quiver with anticipation and desire.

The boy brushed hair of a watery shade from his forehead and looked languorously up and down my body.

And yet it is stupid and simple. I ask him to calculate the

relativistic mass of a single photon. He blinks stupidly, he is flustered, he cannot answer. The ritual has become almost mute—no arcane spray of ash over their bodies could cure them of their pride. They all think I am a beast, a monster with no mind, able only to spout my riddles by rote.

I must explain to him, painstakingly—for I must supply the Answer if he cannot, it the least courtesy I can provide—how the mass of a particle is proportional to its total energy E, and involving the speed of light, c, in the proportionality constant: $m = E/c^2$.

His expression reminds me that occasionally there is beauty to be found in blankness.

And yet, another pair of wooden beads is drawn together, the oil from each mingling, and the weight of my necklace increases. It is for the city planners to worry that the population does not swell, that traders avoid the walls, that no beautiful foreign brides are brought with almond eyes. I fulfill my duty, the coupled words are spoken, and I increase.

This boy sat heavily in my belly, tasting of iodine and oatcakes. I am exhausted of this work, and yet it goes on. I am bombarded by photons with cruel masses, with high cheekbones and stiletto heels. Light sits heavily on my lap, an old whore as bored as her customer is disgusted. But it is the disgust that keeps it going. Disgust, at least, is tangible and real.

If there is a monster there must be a man, or woman, to approach it. It is the way of things. Perhaps when I have brought together all the beads, it will cease to be the way of things. And then I will rest and let Thebes be damned.

DEER BREAK ANTLERS

I-within-Ayako could not breathe. I could not move. Tears rushed from my eyes like a spring from a rock wall, streaming down my cheeks, mixing with sweat and grime from the climb up onto the creaking floor of the third level. My throat was a boulder against a tomb, my limbs a sudden dark wax, flooding into each other, under and around the radiance of the stone figure. I could not think. My mind was empty of everything but it, even the dreams, even the dreams.

Its face, luminous and round as all the suns I have ever known, stared out, beatific, sorrowing, without eyes or mouth. The sorrow penetrated me like a hand, holding my heart, holding all of me that can be moved by beauty, holding me like the mother that died, spilling over with forgiveness. Nothing I had ever done or been or imagined myself mattered, only this ancient stone whose name I could not begin to guess. What god had it been meant to show? I did not know, could not know, but for a slow blink of the sun's eye, it erased every shadow I had dragged behind me like a tawdry merchant's cart, its one broken hand gracefully bent into a mudra of seraphic gentleness.

It made me a child in braids and a poor dress, crawling into my mother's lap and pressing my face into her warm skin. I sobbed against her, my bones cracking open and my deepest blood pouring over her absolving hands. I died away from the dreams. I and the stone were the whole universe, for a moment that stretched out in all directions, an infinite plane of liquid jewels, she was all things, and the smooth gray of its faded eyelids filled my vision with a great burning. All of me was on fire, incandescent, my legs, my mouth, my tears searing as they coursed, rivers of naphtha scalding and cleansing. It was inside me, purging me of all that was not light. I was made of gold, singular, my skin kindled and blazed, I saw nothing at all before me but endless plains of its light and mine flooding together like tributary and river, river and sea.

"Stone," I wept, my face swollen with tears, "tell me a lesson about myself."

Stone considered for a moment, and began.

CICADAS BEGIN TO SING

The cicada lies in the earth for seventeen years. It is warm and dark there, it is soft and wet. Its little legs curl underneath it, and twitch only once in a little while. What does the cicada dream when it is folded into the soil? What visions travel through it, like snow flying fast? Its dreams are lightless and secret. It dreams of the leaves it will taste, it composes the concerto it will sing to its mate. It dreams of the shells it will leave behind, like self-portraits. All its dreams are drawn in amber. It dreams of all the children it will make.

And then it emerges from the earth, shaking dust and damp soil from its skin. It knows nothing but its own passion to ascend—it climbs a high stalk of grass and begins to sing, its special concerto to draw the wing-pattern of its beloved near. And as it sings it leaves its amber skin behind, so that in the end, it has sung itself into a new body in which it will mate, and die.

The cicadas leave their shells everywhere, like a child's lost buttons. The shells do not understand the mating dance that now occurs in the mountains above it. The shell knows nothing of who it has been, it does not remember the *dreaming self, that was warm in the earth. The song emptied it, and now it simply waits for the wind or the rain to carry it away.*

You are the cicada-in-the-earth. You are the shell-in-the-grass. You do not understand what you dream, only that you dream. And when you begin to sing, the song will separate you from your many skins.

This is the lesson of the cicada's dream.

BINDWEED FLOURISHES

I dream that my wrists are bleeding. Mountain spat basalt and bound them. River discovered the village was missing and in his rage tore open the walls of my womb. It lies gaping and red, the marks of his fingers black and terrible. My womb is screaming and they call it music. River says that I am beautiful now. That he will cut more of me open to reveal such beauty. He is planning an expedition to sound the depth of my spinal fluid.

I have had to release my storm clouds and let the oceans lighten. Mountain crushed me under his weight until I yielded. He ground into me grinning and panting. They have poured the foundation of their Palace directly into my throat—mortar and burning pitch, and no I have no voice but the mute growling of my deepest mouth.

I dream that it never ends. There are so many hands inside me now, rummaging in my flesh as though it were an attic. I am vandalized.

They are almost ready to begin the painting of the History in the first Great Hall. I cry silently as they balance the jade vat on the hollow of my throat. River holds the pen as he held my arms, and when he lays it down to rest, I can see it bears the same bruises.

My jaw is broken. The Palace was too large and the first gables shattered the bone. My teeth were scattered like seeds. The villagers scurried to gather them up and return them to River, their rightful owner. But now it will be perfect, and the blood that drips from my earlobe can be used as paint. There is, after all, no sense in waste.

River has only just finished the inscription of their names. That was his proudest task, and it took a long time.

HOT WINDS ARRIVE

I stayed with the statue as long as my belly would allow. The Ayako-body is demanding, however, and soon enough I did not wish to disturb it with the growls of hunger. I descended in sorrow, not knowing if I would have the strength to climb so high again.

I devoured a mash of wild carrots, beans, and mushrooms; I pulled down ripe plums from the branches heavy with green. Mountain provides. The dream-pagoda was inside me then, a bone like any other, and I confess that I had already begun to think on the fourth floor, though I knew my mewling flesh to be to weak to attempt it.

River washed me clean of tears and sweat and blood and dirt. He held me very tenderly in his current, as if I would break into five thousand pieces and float out to the sea. But I did not speak to him, though I could feel his disappointment at not being asked for a lesson in the summer, when he is at his best. River is such a proud creature. He loves display. He had an affair with Moon once, because she shone so prettily on his waters that he fell in love with her. It ended badly.

I had nothing to ask him, my eyes had glazed over like gray water. He became sullen and his banks pouted. I thought of the Stone and how its face had vanished. If none one sees a face, perhaps it is as good as vanished. Perhaps I have no face, either.

The sunlight was thick and hot, pooling on the earth like coils of molten lead. It sat heavily on my eyelids and began its long work of darkening my skin. Off in the Mountain-cliffs, the first cicadas open their amber throats and start to sing, their scream of ecstasy wrapping the air in a soprano fist.

CRICKETS COME
INTO THE WALLS

I dream that I can smell his flesh in the cinnamon-breath of camphor trees. I dream it stops up my nostrils like the spices of the dead. I am mummified by him, each sliver I find takes its correspondent from me.

It is his cheekbone, after all, still hanging with skin and blood like a curtain, drizzling fluid onto my skin. It reeks of river-waste, of rotting crocodile. And yet, I hold his face in my hands again, the high arc of his noble bone-structure, beauty being the mark of divinity.

I dream that the smell of his divinity gags me.

The rains are coming and then it will be harder. His slick-sided flesh will slip from my hands and into the mud-which-swallows. He is my dream-beast, the brother-husband vivisected, the body which was whole now in wet clumps, like hair from a woman's brush. And the smell of it, embalming my body to drag it down with him into the *satori* of dismemberment. I am clay, and his fingers worm their bony lengths into the cracks of my joints, each part of him seeking its mate, but only its mate, having no care for the whole. His cheekbone calls out to mine, begging cartilage to rip from the wicked face.

I am his food. He eats slowly, conserving strength until he can come together again and wrap himself up in river-reeds, in necklaces of ibis-talons, in beast-heads which can be changed to suit the latest fashions. Today it will be Hawk, tomorrow black-tongued Jackal. How beautiful he will be, when the dream is over and he is bodied. My name will be written down in the book of the dead in gold ink, curled vowels and tender penmanship. There will be an asterisk, which notes that I took his place.

THE EAGLEHAWK
STUDIES AND LEARNS

The air is still. It cups me like an older sister's arms and I become slow, languorous, heavy. Mountain has put on his best green, deep and savage, and there are birds circling his gnarled head. Soon, I think to my Ayako-self, the boy will come from the dream-village. Perhaps he will bring me a little chicken whose eggs I could eat. Or even some rice-wine in a clay bottle with a pretty yellow cork.

I haven't seen the moon in weeks. The constant heat-haze, as though from a well-rolled cigarette, prevents it. I am unconnected, removed from light, from the luminal braids that did not tumble down to the fennel and sage, basil and wild mint of an earth where I might have stood if I had not listened to Sparrow and been adopted by Mountain.

Perhaps instead of the fulmination of selves in my heart, I would have made daughters with eyes like plum blossoms. Perhaps I would have had a son with clean fingernails. I would have owned five kimonos, each with a different flower-pattern along the hem. Cherry, lily, chrysanthemum, orchid, peony. There would have been bleating goats and a rooster, even, perhaps, a fine brown horse. There would have been a husband to share a bed, and I would never have built the master-work of my loneliness with such care, the care of a swordsmith or royal architect. I would have kept a little songbird, and learned to play the *koto* with graceful hands.

The moon shines on the woman I never was, on the house I never owned, on her hair like moving water.

ROTTED WEEDS METAMOR-
PHOSE INTO FIREFLIES

I dream that this is the History of the World as River wrote it and Mountain spoke it:

When in the height Heaven was not named, and the Earth beneath did not yet bear a name, all things were Dark and without Law. Into this came Mountain and his brother River, and they brought Light to the World. Mountain saw that a wicked and hideous woman held dominion over Earth, and she was the Mother of Chaos. Mountain saw her, and knew that she was evil, and resolved to deliver Earth from her grasp.

And so in the fullness of Time, through great strength and cunning, it came to pass that Mountain, though her form disgusted him, let himself be seduced by her, for she was also a Harlot. And when he came to lay with her, Mountain contrived it so that River could enter her chamber and bind her at the arms. When the demoness could not move and cried out in her extremity, Mountain drove all the four winds through her belly. He severed her inward parts, he pierced her heart, he overcame her and cut off her life; he cast down her body and stood upon it. And the lord Mountain stood upon her hinder parts, and with his merciless club he smashed her skull.

Mountain shouted his triumph, but the People did not hear, for they had lived in Terror.

So that she could not return and do further evil, Mountain and River devised between them a clever plan. River cut through the channels of her blood, he split her up like a flat fish into two halves; one half of her they established as a covering for heaven; from the other half they fashioned the earth and all its districts. Mountain fixed a bolt; he stationed a watchman, and bade them not to let her Waters come forth. Only River would hold Water beneath his sway, and only Mountain hold Earth. They saw that their Work was Good, and Rested.

This is how the World was made, and how the Men of the World were liberated from the dominion of Evil. So it has been Written, and let no one doubt its Truth.

Dream-tears trickle down my cheeks, and pool on the wheat-bearing valleys below.

THE EARTH IS MUDDY AND THE AIR IS HUMID

The rains have begun. It rained for five days and five nights, battering at my skin even through the slats of the pagoda-floors. Even on the third floor (which is not, after all, so difficult to reach) I cannot escape it, only lie curled around the faceless statue and murmur to it senselessly, words that are all vowels.

And then nothing but the same white haze for days, as though the wind smoked opium, until the belly of heaven opens again and the fat droplets splash down and turn the earth to a sloshing storm of mud and torn branches. Poor Juniper looks bedraggled and his branches have lost their fine berries by the bushel.

Wind conspires with water and I hide away from it. The green on Mountain's flanks looks almost obscene under the footfalls of rain. It is has a glower to it, a strut. Even the cicadas are quiet, a wing-quivering audience for the sky.

Once, when the I-Ayako was younger, we danced in it. Our toes pointed east and the great thick drops fell down onto skin which was perfect, cream-pale and smooth. those were the days when dreams stayed dreams, and did not encroach on the daylight like cities on the forest. Our/my hair spun around me in a long fan, my toes wriggled in the soft mud. Those were the days when I loved my lessons, and I laughed wide-mouthed at the pearl-silver sky:

"Rain! Tell me a lesson about dancing!"

Even the bamboo sways when the wind visits.

In those days, the voice of the rain was young and sweet.

THE GREAT RAINS
SWEEP THROUGH

I dream I range over the seas, above the hyphen of rain clouds. I see my dream-sister on the bone-islands, her hands in the chalky soil, trying to force her crops to grow. River tries to help her, he flows around her, through her sugar cane and orange trees, through her banana groves and her copses of dark-leaved mango. All of these have withered and turned black, and I can see her beat her red fists against the earth-that-was-me and weep terrible tears.

She has set up a temple, fine and white, with a shaded veranda—heaps of hibiscus and palm fronds pile up the altar. There is a thickly sweet smell as they rot, trickling a sickly red juice onto the clean floor. She preaches there, and calls herself the fire-god who kindled the first flame when the world was dark. She tells River she never had a sister, that she was an only child, that mother and father loved her too much to have another. She demands that she is beautiful and that pigs be roasted in her honor.

But still, her groves will not grow. My bones would not let such a thing occur, that my sister would eat the fruit of my body. Still, the dream-rot spoils everything she touches.

It is no matter to me—better that she destroyed my flesh, that I am now naked of it and a flame alone. But I pity her. She rages, scarlet hair flying behind her, clutching handfuls of the bone-soil and ripping her breaths in half. I care little; she is a mewling puppet stuttering in her temple, her aspect mawkish and dull. I am grateful for her stones, which made me the lover of cities, which took my flesh and left only the fire.

I shrug garnet shoulders and move on. It is of no concern.

THE COOL WIND ARRIVES

The sweat on my neck has dried. I eat mustard greens and the beans which by now are thick and lantern-green.

There is a kind of contentment to be found in the dream-hermitage—it comes only when the solitude-temple is built and the hermit is interred there, but it does come.

It is in the earthy tang of harvested vegetables.

It is in the smell of the mildewed pagoda-floors.

It is in the little bells of River singing by, and the heft of silence under Mountain, who carves his shape out of the void-that-is-sky.

It is the ants milling redly home with prizes of berry and sap.

It is pale petals stuck to the bottom of my left sandal, dew-damp and wrinkled.

It is Moon touching River tenderly, her hand heavy with the memory of their lovemaking.

It is the dark, earthy taste of persimmons and the fire-orange of their skin.

It is the sound of herons washing downstream, the sound of their blue feathers rubbing together like cricket's legs.

It is the song of the plovers in the scented trees.

It is the shade of the pagoda at noon, the shapes that its shape casts on the earth.

It is the thick-dropped rain playing in the mud.

It is in bare feet that tunnel in loose soil, and the hum of cicadas which is like monks repeating their syllable endlessly into the hot nights.

But it is easily disturbed.

WHITE DEW DESCENDS

I dream that this time it is a girl. She comes to trade her
water-jars in the great market, and indeed, they are skill-
fully shaped, with elegant spouts and handles that curve
backwards like the necks of water-birds.

It is all the same to me whether her hair is the color of a
burned oak or of the fire that burned it. But like all my
postulants, she is beautiful. She smells of alfalfa and licorice. I feel a question-bead slide down the strand, and its
passing sounds a baritone note, deep and wide as a bell.

"Monster," she speaks first, which is unheard of, not
done— "may I ask you a question first?"

I dream that I consider it. Of course, it merely prolongs
the ritual. But she is lovely, and it will not save her, so there
is no harm. I nod my golden head, and the sand-choked curls
of my mane tumble forward.

"What walks on four legs in the morning, six in the afternoon, and none in the evening?"

My dream-laughter fills the desert and I am sorry for a
moment that I will have to devour her. I want to caress her
cheek instead, and feed her from my own mouth, as if she
were my cub.

"Why, I do, child. For in infancy I walk on my four paws, in maturity I add my two wings to this, and in old age I creep on my belly and use none of these. That was a good riddle, girl. I shall remember it."

Disappointment rakes it fingers across her face. I can see that this was her plan, to win her entrance by becoming herself the monster, and reversing the natural order. But such plans are not to be. The face of the coin cannot be its reverse. I am to far beneath the earth to be troubled by such small movements.

"And now for mine," I intone, in my richest voice. The girl squares her feet as though she is to recite a verse, and shakes her hair like a broom tangled in cobwebs. "If n is a whole number greater than 2, prove for me that there are no whole numbers a, b, c such that $a^n + b^n = c^n$?"

I dream that my smile is fat and sated, knowing she cannot answer and that the sweet smell of her skin will soon be inside me.

The girl's eyes fill with prismatic tears. She understands. Any answer she might make would be a fantasy of foolishness. And instead of stuttering a guess, she simply walks to me, puts her tiny hand on my flank, moving her fingers in the thick fur with a thoughtful grace.

The dream-girl lies down beneath me, willingly, and exposes her white throat to my mouth. Her tears slide off of her cheeks and onto the dry sand, onto the strands of her hair.

I dream that I weep as I swallow her.

THE EVENING CRICKET CHIRPS

Everywhere, on every high stalk of yarrow or fennel, on every low branch of camphor or juniper, even on the outcroppings of the dream-pagoda, the cicadas are leaving their shells.

Each one is perfect, unbroken, clinging to the stalk it has chosen with total abandonment. They must know such rapture as they wriggle out, and the grass rubs their bellies while the whole sky sings.

I think on what the Stone taught me as I watch them. I can never quite catch them at it, I only see the translucent shell cast off, with delicate mandibles and a diamond thorax. Some strange-eyed goddess has cast off her jewelry, and my meadow is full of sparking gems. The sun shines through them and they become little lanterns attending a nameless festival, swaying merrily from their stalks while the wind gossips with the flowers. They have sung themselves empty; the melody took their souls. The dream-shells remain, little urns empty of ash.

There was a moment when I wanted to gather them up and burn them in a pyre, to honor their lives under the ground and wish them well in their mating. But I could not. It seemed wrong to touch them.

They are planning a Palace of my teeth. Molar-turrets, inci-sor-halls, portcullis of canines. When it is finished it will block my throat and I will never speak again.

They are familiar to me, as though each of these cara-paces is a mirror rimmed in bronze, to show the lesson of the cicada's dream: that I am deep in the earth and dreaming, and it is the seventeenth year.

THE EAGLEHAWK
SACRIFICES BIRDS

River has seen my tears; I dream they anger him. He washes up roughly against my face to clean them from the skin which is still beautiful and green. His whitecaps like scalpels cut the salt from my ducts, trying to stop them up entirely. But he cannot do it.

He calls on Mountain, who fashions blinders from his shale rock, and places them over my eyes. I cannot see to the side, only straight down the ridge of my nose to the half-built Palace. It is coming along, now, since they painted the History. Great crimson turrets rise up, exactly the shade of my lips—and in fact they have sliced away layers of lip to make a deep-colored pigment for the portcullis. I am being torn down to the bone, and it must come soon, if the conspiracy of my limbs is to come at all.

This is the architecture of affliction, the cryptogram of the palace stairs whispers that no freedom is possible, no surcease can be salvaged from the flotsam of my quarried body. Boils erupt on skin that once did not bear up under the roots of houses. This is the dream of desecration, the dream of the palace building. This is the first body, which foaled all other bodies in an unimaginable stable. It can be seen as though it were tattooed on a woman's stomach—the line of bodies, connected like a chain of paper dolls, from the one the Mountain harmed to the one the Mountain loves. A shock of limbs move between us, rimmed in light.

In my own body which is not my own I palpitate and sweat great oak barrels of chianti. I weep retsina and bleed a late harvest riesling. The drops well on my fingertips like rain—small lips fasten to me, drawing the vintage from my pores. I sit in a basket of lies like oranges and pears, building, too, the architectures of pain and vengeance.

HEAVEN AND EARTH
TURN STRICT

When I was a child and Ayako only, the village had a great number of silkworms, and the women wove with radiance. The fat little grubs ate such beautiful things in order to make silk in the ovens of their bodies—white mulberry, wild orange, watery lettuce. They were coddled like tiny emperors. Perhaps my gentleman-Moth was once a silkworm, for when the time came that they metamorphosed into moths and had mated, the worms were forgotten and shooed from the house as a nuisance.

I can remember one autumn when they all became sick, for the mulberry crop was sour and fouled that year. They did not produce the pure white fluid that dried into the fine thread which then could be wound into a delicate rose-shade, even dyed indigo or emerald. From their translucent worm-bodies came only a thick black fiber, which was not even or pure, but knotted and bunched in places, so that it caused the poor things great pain to expel the viscous, wet silk. In my child-dreams I heard them screaming as their ashen bellies were torn out by masses of dark, coiled rope.

It did not dry properly, and so the women burned it all in a great heap with the bodies of the silkworms which had died giving birth to the death-thread. When they caught flame the smell of flesh and cloth burning was like white cardamom crushed in a china pot.

The ashes blew away with the next wind and the silkworm colony healed itself.

Yet I have always wondered—what marvelous, secret things could have been woven from that wet, black thread, the thread that smelled so sweet burning?

RICE RIPENS

I dream that I am kneeling on the riverbank, vomiting into the clear water. In one hand I hold his leg, severed at the knee, and tears have mixed with bile and silt-water to make a horrible stew.

I can see on the kneecap a tiny white scar where he cut himself shaving, and I kissed the blood away. I remember the copper taste in my mouth, the taste of his inward self, his red blood swimming in me.

And now I have a surfeit of his blood. I carry it in buckets and in water-jars balanced on my head. I carry it in wine-sacks and water-bladders, in thatched baskets and even in my cupped hands. I did not think a man could have so much blood, even him.

I dream the brother-husband with his sundered body. I dream I see him in the moon which drives the sky before it like chariot-horses. I dream the corpse forming around me, the *homunculus* of his disparate parts, graying and moldered, and I have no thread to sew them.

What sort of golem will rise up out of this collected flesh with *emet* tattooed on its palm? Will I have to whisper in his wizened ear, wet and wrinkled as a newborn, some arcanity to bring it surging together? Will it love me still?

I dream it will not.

I dream I will not see the golem-husband whole.

All my eye can see is my own shape hunched over the river, emptying my own body of itself.

THE WILD GEESE COME

Feet crunched on the pebble-path to my pagoda. The heart within the Ayako-body leapt up like a fish flashing in the sun. The dream of the village-boy has come!

And he did come, walking up the Mountain path in a simple shift with a polished walking-stick, carrying a leather pack on his shoulders. He was not the same boy—I did not expect it—but he was handsome and strong and I was eager to speak to him.

The boy caught sight of me and a look of horror stole into his black eyes. For a moment I saw myself as I must have appeared to him: an old witch-ghost in tattered rags with horse-like hair that stuck out in black and gray bolts, filled with twigs and leaves and river-reeds. My bones were visible beneath skin that was too pale, and the hands which reached out to welcome him must have seemed like death-claws.

I do not know where she comes from, the crone that sneaks into the house and steals girlhood away.

Hurriedly, the boy lays out his gifts on the damp grass: a sack of new rice, tea leaves folded into a blue cloth, a pouch containing dried lentils and a chunk of pork fat. It was a treasure—each year the gifts were better, and within my

Ayako-heart I was happy, for I knew this meant my old home prospered.

I called after the boy as he turned his feet to run—but not too fast, lest the ghost be angered—back to the village.

"Wait, Boy," I rasped. This time, I was sure, I knew the way to trap the dream of the clean-finger nailed child and make him stay. He would help me take down the timbers of my solitude. "Let me tell you a lesson about the Mountain."

He paused. The young can rarely resist a lesson. They pretend to loathe them, but in their secret hearts a good lesson is sweeter to them than winter cakes. He looked back to me and whispered, his voice full of terror, "All...all right."

I crept up to him, the first human I had spoken to since the men with the iron clothes burned the village. "What you see is not Mountain. It is the dream that Mountain dreams."

The boy squinted skeptically in the late afternoon sun, which rumbled a pleasant orange-gold.

"Are you the Old Woman on the Mountain or the dream that she dreams?"

"Your guess is as good as mine, young one. I am old, and I live on the Mountain, so it is possible that I am she. I possess three floors of a pagoda and a bean patch. What do you possess?"

"A colt, which will one day be a horse," the boy replied, "and a black rooster with yellow eyes. The rest belongs to my father and will be mine when I am grown. But why do you possess only three floors?"

"I am too weak to reach the top," I admitted, ashamed again for the bulging veins and jaundiced fingernails I also possessed.

"Then why not just try for the fourth? Four is more than three. Perhaps then your guess will be better. My father teaches that the more a man possesses, the wiser he is."

I laughed quietly, and the chuckle was a hoarse and empty one. "Then your father must be very wise."

The boy looked strangely at me and I saw his heart decide to speak no more. He bowed and retreated down the Mountain, with the sun on his back. I did not have the heart to try to stop him again.

SWALLOWS RETURN

Into the belly of the sun, my eyes burn to white oil and threads of flame spin down to the earth. I dream that my hunger gnashes its own heart, searching for a city as beautiful as a tinderbox, a city to lie over and sigh into its towers.

I dream that the autumn has passed while I danced in the laps of a dozen mountains, throwing my hands through their rooftops. In the fire-dream, all things burn under me, and the scorching of all things smells sweet.

On the horizon, I can see a great wall. It is a hundred shades of gold and its gate is strong. A wide plain stretches before it that might have once been green, but pitched battles have stained it red and black. It is a city by the sea, dark as wine, and sleek black ships line its harbor like suitors. Warriors are pressing against the wall, a bronze wave breaking on stone. Its towers are coquettish and tall, slim as girls, beckoning.

I can smell incense burning desperately in temples, I can smell terror-sweat in seven hundred bedrooms. I can hear the dull thud of marching men, and the squall of the dying. I can hear women weeping, and the rustle of their dresses on marble floors. The great wall whispers that it would welcome me, that it would show me new pleasures of which I had not yet had the courage to dream.

I feel my mouth water, and drops of oily flame begin to fall from my body.

Soon.

FLOCKS OF BIRDS
GATHER GRAIN

This time I spent an hour stuck between the third and fourth levels, limbs splayed like some distended, helpless spider. There were no more footholds at that height and the distance between floors had seemed only to grow. Excruciatingly I inched sideways, my hips aching, to a thick vine that hung against the wall.

Touching it, I breathed deeply and trusted my weight to its length. Instead of a spider I then hung in the cavernous tower like the rope to a grotesque bell. And slowly, hand over hand, I raised myself up along the green stalk until the fourth level passed beneath me and I could see the tracks of ancient footprints in the dust. I let go shakily and stood in the center of a room which was almost intact. I had come through a large hole in the floor but other than that chasm, the wood was smooth and deeply oiled.

And in the center of the grained wood lay a book.

It was strangely bound, not in a scroll as I knew books to be, but clasped in a leather casing which was not black, but dark from the sweat-thick attentions of many hands. It had no design or picture, it had only the clutch of cream-yellow paper within its jaws.

It bulged slightly, a fat heart on the upbeat.
On the cover it read in yellowing ink:
This is the Book of Dreams.

THUNDER SUPPRESSES HIS VOICE

What is a Riddle? It is not merely a word game, or a puzzle, or a even, truly, a question. It is a series of locks which open only onto each other, in a great circle that leads back to a Truth—and this is the secret I tell you now on the great wall of Thebes: the Truth is always in the Question, never in the answer. All conceivable truths are in a single question. If I ask a boy-child to tell me my name, I have already told him the ancient truth that a name holds power. I have told him that I am more than a monster, for I possess a name. I have told him that in names lies the path to freedom, not only of the body, but of the ineffable Self. All this I have told him, before I ever demanded such a simple repayment as an answer, if only he could listen. There is not nearly so much gold in the answer, which is nothing more than a word.

What is a Riddle?

It is a box full of satisfactions. It never fails the questioner or the respondent. When it is opened, there is a soft intake of breath, when it remains closed, breath itself is stopped.

And on this box is written:

This is the Book of Dreams.

BURROWING BEETLES WALL UP
THEIR DOORS WITH EARTH

I am afraid to open it. A closed book is beautiful, because anything can be written in it, and so everything is. All the stories that ever were—love, honor, death, lust, wisdom—every word written is contained inside it as long as the I-that-is-Ayako does not reach forward to open the cover and reveal what *is* actually written there. It can only be disappointing. Perhaps that is why it bulges, so full of what it *could* be. The curve of potential, like a pregnant woman's belly.

An open book is ugly, it is splayed open like a whore. It can only be what it is.

I am afraid of it, I do not want to touch it. It does not fill me with light like the Stone or the goat's milk. What do I need with a book of dreams when dreams people my body as though I were a capital-city?

WATERS DRY UP

River is worried. He sees that my dream-tears continue, falling with more speed, pooling around my shoulders in a salty ring. River is usually the first to understand. He will not tell Mountain until he is sure he cannot punish me alone. He set the sun on me to dry them, but the tears are alive now, they run their course like the mewling children of River do, heedless and wild. They come and come and come.

Within myself, I am smiling.

He himself tries to wash them away, frothing under their weight, blue on blue. But they sink within him and he cannot move to stop up my eyes like wine bottles. I am heavier, heavier by far. My salts scald and bruise him—I am warmed by his screams.

He sets the wind to dry them, but they can only soak up the thick waters, and send them earthward again as rain. The dams begin to swell up with my sorrows, the sea is black and deep. Great storms erupt on the hipbones of Mountain, drenching his gray skin with borrowed tears.

He set the glaciers on me to freeze them, but they are hot and thick, rolling over my body in a great gray slough, over my dark-treed belly, the skin of boughs that covers my secret womb, and on this skin is written in the sap and tears:

This is the Book of Dreams.

WILD GEESE COME AS GUESTS

I dream I have found the last of him. In the deep river currents where no reeds grow it floated like an abandoned cradle. I am ready now, to take the river into me. I do not want to, but now there can be no more delays, and I can see the colors of the water changing. I am draped in his body—intestines, blood, leg, clavicle, cheek, eyes, jaw, scalp, hands, skin, spleen, heart, skull. I am dressed for the ball, for a second wedding, for the insensate ritual of taking my dream-husband's corpse into myself.

I know what is coming, what the river will leave in me like sandy deposits in the delta. I am resigned, I want it done. I want to leave it on the banks and never think on it again. The hawk-headed child looms large in my vision. I can feel its feathers already prickling the walls of my womb.

I stifle revulsion as I clean the last of the dream-husband's organs in the cool river, which has inundated the valley and given life to the amaranth crops. I am the body of the sky, and I will give birth to light from light. I cannot tell if it is still a dream. If the child I will take from his mute body will be a dream-son or if he will be real. I am the amaranth, and I am the river.

I hold the last of him in my hands, mottled gray and shot with hardened blood. And on its length is written:

This is the Book of Dreams.

SPARROWS DIVE INTO THE WATER BECOMING CLAMS

Metamorphosis. It is a long line of bellies, chained together flesh-wise, circling each other in a blood-black smear. A book is a belly, too. It is full of dark, nameless things decaying into each other, dissolving in acid, jostling for position. Kingfishers dive into the water and become women; women dive into the earth and become books.

What woman was this book before it grew its leather wings? I do not want to disturb her, to open her and pry out her secrets with a knife.

I was breathing heavily, trying to escape the book without moving. Perhaps peace lay in it, perhaps not. I did not want to know. I wanted my bean patch and my first floor. I wanted River and Mountain sleeping beside me in the dark.

I knew then I would not open it. I knew my story, I did not need the book. I would not harm it, its capacity for infinite wisdom, by reading what was truly there. I was not sure, I reasoned, that I *could* read any longer.

But I could not stop looking at it, the vulgarity of its bulging cover. I wanted it, like a barren woman wants a child. I would leave it, let it remain quiet and alone, as I have been for so long. Let the scholars in Kyoto pour over pages until their eyes dribble onto their cheeks. I took my lessons from Gate and Moth, Goat and River, and Mountain, above all my patron Mountain, who held me in his arms and whispered lullabies.

I stood before the book. I was the anatomy of a *no*. All of me cried out in rejection of the black heart of the dream-pagoda.

I had to escape it. Up. Up onto the fifth floor, where there would be no terrible book to make my sinews tear themselves like so much paper.

CHRYSANTHEMUMS
ARE TINGED YELLOW

I dream that I begin to seduce the city. I touch its walls lightly, with a fingertip. I brush my lips over the ramparts. I am better now, I know how to make the fire last. I know how to take my pleasure from a city.

Before the Gate a dream-battle is raging. Armor has fallen in the dirt made mud by the glut of black blood, bodies are piled up to be burned. Two men are slashing at each other, their faces turned into masks of beasts, theatre-clay with fleshy ribbons. The rest of the army looks on, waiting on the outcome. The only sounds are the cheap, hollow ring of swords, the dull thud of blows landing on leather-wrapped shields, and the hush of my body moving over the bricks of the city.

My nipples dip into the fountains and they are dried, my hair falls over a siege tower and it crashes to the frothing earth. I laugh and laugh. What they battle over is already mine. I have claimed it.

And on the great carved gate is written:
This is the Book of Dreams.

In the fire-dream, all things burn under me, and the scorching of all things smells sweet.

THE WOLF SACRIFICES
THE BEASTS

The fifth floor was perfect. I simply climbed up a ladder which had not a single rung broken, and stood in the center of a room with no cracks in the floor, no pockmarks on the walls—even the paintings were untouched. They showed strange and terrible things—a beast sitting atop a low wall, half lion and half eagle, with the face of a woman. A woman tied to the earth with a green-walled palace built in her mouth. A woman standing in a river much vaster than my little creek, with the severed organs of some nameless man draped over her body. A woman whose skin flamed red, sighing onto a city which caught flame from her breath.

And in the corner stood a small Fox, beautifully auburn and cream-furred, with pert ears and a gentle snout, sitting on her haunches with an expression on her face which in the world of foxes must have passed for a smile.

"Why did you not open the book?" she asked softly, in a cultured, harmonious voice which rustled through the room like a veil blown from the shoulders of some pretty child.

"I did not want to disturb it," I gulped, suddenly ashamed at my cowardice.

"If I brought it here now, would you change your mind?"

I considered it, thought back on the dark oils of its cover. "No. I would rather you tell me lessons. I would rather Gate spoke to me under the stars."

"But there are no lessons in it. Only a story."

"My story?" I whispered.

"In a way. It is the story of your dream-women. In it are written their names."

The Fox scratched at her cupped red ear. "They have no names. Only the hermit-Ayako has a name," I protested.

"It is only that you do not know their names. But if you do not open the book, you will not finish the dreams, you will not reach the sea. Do you not recall what the Sphinx said? All women are one woman. If you do not seek out the shells they leave behind, you will not shed your own." The Fox trotted over and stood before me.

"Who are you? Why are you here at the top of my tower?" I rasped, my voice dry as rice in the sun.

"I have many names, as you do. This is my pagoda, I have always been here. I am the Stone, too. Once it bore my face. I am Mercy, I am Compassion. I am the flowing water that carries you. You cannot step into me twice, and yet, each of your footsteps drags four behind them. I am nothing more than a door through which you will pass. I am here to show you the End."

FOLIAGE TURNS
YELLOW AND FALLS

Outside the dream-pagoda, leaves drifted down with thoughtless grace, green, gold, brown. The air had sharpened, swallows sang down the sun.

"Is this the dream of the Fox? Or the dream of the Fifth Floor?" I asked.

"In all probability. I have no revelations for you, only the peace that comes with understanding. You did not strive to reach the top of the pagoda—you fled to the pinnacle without thought of ascension. Because you did not seek it, it is yours. You dive into the water and become a clam, a pheasant, a book. This is about metamorphosis—this is about solitude. Look how you have built your temple! Look how high and bright the spires!" The Fox laughed, a deep sound in her throat like skin being stretched over a drum. "You must listen to the dream of the Sphinx. She tells the truth—she cannot do otherwise. Her body carries the physiognomy of true things—only a true answer will ease her hunger. Thus, she is emptiness. Not the expanse of pure emptiness in which wisdom grows, but the gnawing absence of knowledge, that which burns."

"But are all these women me?" I begged, confused.

"All women are one woman. You are the I-that-is. They are the I-that-is-possible. Open the book, and follow the voice-threads where they lead. Out of the black silk harvest they came, and they are yours. You have a responsibility to them. The multiplied "I" can not be reduced back into itself until all its light-paths have been followed. The Sphinx would say this has already happened. If it has, it should not be difficult for you."

And the book lay between us, bulging and dark, promising. The Fox retained her beatific face; I opened the cover with a careful hand and read these things:

INSECTS TUCK THEMSELVES AWAY

If all women are one woman who has already lived out each of her infinite possible lives, if all their stories are already told, if, in fact, all possible events have already occurred, the one infinitely copied photon has completed all conceivable pathways, then we approach not only the unfortunate conclusion that all Riddles have already been asked and answered, but must accept that we reside in the Wasteland of Quantum Exhaustion.

"Do you like that, Oedipus? I am delivering a paper on the subject at a conference in Alexandria next month," the dream-Sphinx mused, and Prince Oedipus picked his teeth with a sliver of bone. He is bored.

In the Wasteland of Quantum Exhaustion, the woman-who-is-all-women would stand at a central point, one of her possible selves would be a commonality around which other possible selves would revolve. Of course, each of the women in then in and of herself a commonality, and thus there is no center per se to the system, only an infinitely expanding series of centers, which negates the idea of a center altogether. As we all know, a center cannot be within the system and govern it simultaneously.

On the other hand, the wavelength of each potential self is determined by its distance from the fulcrum-crone. But if we understand any of an infinite series of women and ur-women to be fulcra, the wavelength of each self is impossible to determine, being both identical with and impossibly far from its point of origin. In the yolk-riddled void, these photon-bodies float, flashing red and blue, containing within them all possible redness and blueness, joining together like spinning gears, and at each notch exploding into a third (or fifth, or eleventh,) mirror-self, gashing the darkness in its birth pangs—a wash of pure, white light.

"I don't think you are listening to me," the dream-Sphinx said crossly. "Have you solved the Riddle yet? I think I have given you plenty of time. What goes on four legs in the morning, two in the afternoon, and three in the evening? It isn't even a very good Riddle. You should have heard the last one."

Suddenly, the Prince's rather dull face lit up with revelation.

"I do!" he cried, leaping to his feet, "I do! A man does, I mean."

And the Sphinx smiled.

"Don't congratulate yourself too much. It isn't the Riddle after all, that you have conquered, but the Riddle that conquers you."

Oedipus did not even do her the honor of eating her, but rather stabbed her with his dagger and watched her die with the peculiar satisfaction of aristocracy. He left her corpse to the flies and the desert-birds. And her body was the color of the dream-sand, which even as she bled began to cover her in gold, and preserve her bones as relics.

As she died, the dream-Sphinx uttered her last Riddle, which is, of necessity, unanswerable.

Of course, Oedipus, your story is already told, too. The King is dead, the Queen is dead, your daughters and sons are dead, and you are blinded on the road to Colonus. This is as easy to read as an answer in the back of a mathematics textbook. It has already been a hundred times over, a thousand. There can be no free will in the Wasteland. We are all bound up together, belly to belly to belly.

When one possible woman dies, it is as though a shutter closes, and the light from a certain window is snuffed out. There are many, many more windows, and really, since the window had already been opened and shut an infinite number of times, since in potential it occupies both the states of Open and Shut, nothing changes at all. Is this process indefinite?

WATER BEGINS TO FREEZE

"I do not want to, Fox. Just tell me my lesson. They are mine, I do not like to see them written. They are my own, no one else's."

"The more you possess, the wiser you become?" Fox asked, with an arch expression. I blushed.

"I did not say I was wise."

"This is the way. Each by each, night falls and the rivers freeze over, the black branches gather ice, the seeds sleep in the earth and dream the peculiar dreams of rooted things. The cicadas stop singing, the crickets die. You are not separate from this. Stories end, riddles are answered. If there is no end, no story has been told. Though the answers to a single riddle are infinite, the number of correct answers is finite—there is but one. I am the answer to you. I am the second bead, that which completes your question."

Night had stolen up the side of the pagoda, twisted dark fingers into the vines, and now shone blackly across the floor.

"Then the I-that-is-Ayako is the true thing. The others are false," I concluded with sorrow.

"In the end, silk-child, does it matter which is which?"

"To me, it matters," I pleaded.

"When it does not, then you will be wise." The Fox licked her paw and gestured towards me. "Turn the page," she said softly.

EARTH BEGINS TO FREEZE

There is an old circus trick: a girl lets a serpent swallow her whole. Beautiful people pay their pennies and see a woman become the apple of Eden, devoured by the grinning dragon, writhingly slick with olive oil so that when the tattered red curtains shut, her partner can haul her feet-first from those hinged jaws, a grotesque, hermaphroditic birth enacted every night at seven and nine o'clock sharp. This act requires both the serpent and the girl's consent—neither can perform it without the other. The old serpent lets herself be abused by the lovely woman and the crowd, but in exchange, she enjoys the bliss of reliving the meal over and over again.

In the audience, perhaps a mother will whisper to her child, "That was how the old stories say it was in the beginning of the world, when Tiamat, who was Queen of the Watery Abyss, was destroyed and the earth made from her flesh. She was swallowed by the serpent, too."

But I was not. I was the serpent and the girl. Mountain was the circus-master.

Now it is quiet. I have covered Mountain. I have covered

River. I have flooded the hallways of the Palace and erased the History of the World. The ink itself has dissolved in me until no creature can taste its sourness. I spat the castle from my mouth when the floods came.

The salt-flood of my tears cleansed the world—the abyss is on the face of the earth now, and at last there is quiet. The waters rushed in and the dams broke with a sound like matchsticks snapping, the foam hushed over my belly and my hair floated on the waves like a silver-knotted net. There was a tumult of sea, the great salt waves erasing villages, temples, towns, capitals. It made everything clean, transcendent, pure. When the Moon rose up over the surface of the earth and saw the New Sea, she exulted in her diamond carriage and cried out with her voice of spun glass.

I battered Mountain with waves and forced River to join his water to mine. Mountain is merely buried, his voice shut up in a blue casket—River is within me, and I relive the meal over and over, with delight. He twists in my belly with delicious fervor.

There is flotsam everywhere, but that will pass. Seabirds call out desolate songs and search for aeries that have long been swallowed. They roost now on anything that is buoyant—cradles, spinning wheels, stable doors. That will pass, too. The world will be made again, no doubt. It is the way. The process is indefinite. It is made, it is dismantled, it is made again. Perhaps this time I will make it, and write my name in crushed jade.

I am peaceful now, the peace of the full belly. I look out over the sea and watch my wounds heal themselves. Flesh knits itself to itself, slowly, slowly. I am still missing many teeth, but I have confidence that they will turn up. I can afford contentment, I have bought it dearly.

Half of my body is still hung in the sky like a trophy. I lie on the earth-that-is-me and stare into the sky, which stares back. And we rock ourselves to sleep, we two, in this infinite mirror.

Softly, Mountain rumbles beneath me.

PHEASANTS DIVE INTO THE WATER BECOMING MONSTER CLAMS

In the dream of Ayako, she touches the book with tender hands and the Fox watches her. In the dream of Ayako she is washed in moonlight scented by the sea. It is becoming very cold, and Mountain has drawn over himself his old snow-cloak. In the dream of Ayako, her hands are terribly thin and have begun, in places, to shine blue and indigo.

In the dream of Ayako, the thought has begun to form in her that none of the women are real, that even she is a shade, a vision. Perhaps the villagers are right to think her a vengeful ghost. Perhaps the village is not real, either. She had, of course, long suspected that the boys who brought her rice were dreams. This thought was like the grain of sand that forces the oyster to make a pearl—it pained her, and yet the fist of her soul closed around it.

Perhaps the dream at the base of her soul was true—the silent girl who did not move. But perhaps not. Ships existed that had no anchors, perhaps even that had no sails or oars. It was possible that she existed with nothing at her core but ether, nothing but a dark swirl of air.

129

In the dream of Ayako, the Fox lies down beside her in the weak light, her red haunches glittering. She is very lovely, with her grand tail. Ayako thinks that the Fox must have found a great many succulent mice to keep her this fat in the swift-snowed winter.

And because Ayako is lonely, she reads aloud, simply so that she may hear the voice of a human, whether or not she is real.

THE RAINBOW HIDES

In the ninth month of pregnancy the fetus is nearly fully grown. It has gained a great deal of subcutaneous fat and can normally breathe outside the womb at this stage. The mother will experience anxiety and discomfort in the weeks prior to birth. The fetus sleeps for the majority of its tenancy in the womb, and experiences REM sleep, an indication of dreaming.

I kneel in the deep water to give birth, to finish the course he decided for me. In a dream did I mount the golem-husband and take the child into my belly. In a dream did I swell like a bow drawing and feel the hawk-headed son stir in my womb, felt the hard press of his talons against my flesh. Feathers serrate the uterine walls, and the metallic beak kneads my flesh like meager bread. In a dream did I set the body into a sarcophagus of jasper and agate, and let it sail into the south on the great currents.

And now I kneel in the silt, attended by crocodiles with their pupilless eyes, and my body drains out of itself—water and blood and pages of dedicated verse. I have lost the dream-husband, even his desiccated flesh is lost to me. I replace him with the dream-son and hope that I am not asked to sew his bones back together with the threads of my hair, as I have had to do with his father.

I cry out to the desert and my voice is eaten by a dearth of wind. My belly cuts itself like a flayed fish; a bloody-eyed child crawls out and shakes amniotic fluid from his feathered hair. Sobbing, I reach for him over the ruin of my body, clutching my son with the moon between his brow, little Horus, who will make the world over again.

I fall backwards into exhaustion, and my blood eddies out into the Nile. It is promptly devoured by a school of infant catfish, and the sun begins to rise in the west.

HEAVEN'S ESSENCE RISES UP AND EARTH'S ESSENCE SINKS DOWN

"This is the last woman," the Fox said, and I knew it was true. I was not the last woman, of course. I was not the first. The I-that-is-Ayako is a hinge which opens and shuts strange windows, who dreams she is more than her flesh.

"Words are redundancies, after all, my girl. Mountain abides. River changes. The cicada sings its time and is silent. All these things can be known without a single word. You have been glutted with words, but I have opened up a drain at the base of your heart and soon you will be empty as an amber shell. It is not altogether a sad thing."

I, and all the dreams of myself, looked in one body out the window of the pagoda, at the striated skin of Mountain, gray and quartz-white, as though he had been weeping. The blue-gold light of dawn crept up his flank, pressing his velvet nose into the stone. The sky had dropped its hazy veils over the valley, and to sit in the center of the morning was to sit *zazen* in the center of some vast pearl. The trees had all become bare again, and my garden was a patch of black soil, concealing the dreaming seeds.

As I turned the last page of the book and began to read, Fox extended her rosy tongue until it nearly touched my face. And on it, like a jewel, was a single, perfect cicada shell.

WALLING OURSELVES UP,
IT BECOMES WINTER

The man who was killed they called the breaker of horses, and the one who killed him dragged his body behind a chariot around the walls of the city. The sweat of the brown horses ran thick and fast, and the fire-goddess drew back from the holy city, so stunned was she by the madness of two men. The charioteer had driven himself into a frenzy—his hair flew wildly as a ship's loose sail, his teeth gnashed, his knuckles were white on the reins. Women tore their hair and begged him to stop, but even as the wheels splintered into wedges and two of the horses dropped dead of exhaustion, he would not cease.

The city trembled at the sound of the careening hoof beats, and the fire-goddess bided her time.

But I lay over the city and it rose to meet the movements of my crimson body—I only had to wait a little while. It crackled through my fingers and the mortar itself exploded into flame, the towers thrust up into me and fell back scorched to dust. I laughed and wept as my skin covered the walls and courtyards, the markets and temples. The wind whipped along the ramparts and the flames arched towards the pure white sky. The swords themselves melted to a bronze wine, running freely over the cobbled streets.

I lay in the center of it, curled into myself like a yin-yang, pulsing with heat, smiling into my belly and reveling in the surrender of the city to my love. Soon it would be a smoking black ruin, a diorama of ash that had once been called sacred.

But now was the best time, when I shot my flames into the windy towers and consumed the flesh of my body and the flesh of the divine city with one great, red mouth. This was my finest work, my masterpiece, the conflagration of cityflesh and horseflesh and manflesh. I could smell the hair of consecrated virgins sizzling, the paint bubbling on their altars, blood cooking into the walls. Over and over the city swore itself to me, gave itself over, abandoned its body into my arms. The tombs that ringed the citadel like a pretty necklace became pyres, and within the spiced smoke I suffered my scarlet paroxysms of luminosity.

When it was over, and the city lay steaming black on its high bluff, when the sea thunders it funereal march, I watched the last timbers cave inward, the last sparks gutter in the dawn wind.

I bent my roseate face and kissed gently the blessed ruin before turning away.

THE COPPER PHEASANT
CEASES ITS CALL

In the dream of Ayako, there is a pagoda-tower. It is empty. There is no wine-sack. There is no statue whose face has been erased by centuries. There is no Fox with kind eyes. There is no Book. There is no hint of what has or has not passed within it, only the jagged hole in the roof through which unimaginable stars have shone, and which now lets through the first shafts of winter light, falling like snow through the tower.

There is an old woman, curled up like a child, on the floor of the uppermost level, whose rags flutter in the breeze. The sunlight makes her skin translucent, shows the blown glass of her bones and the delicate network of stilled veins.

There is no breath, and her lips are the color of the frozen river parting to receive her steps.

TWE TIGER BEGINS TO ROAM

In the village, the boy whose lot it had been to bring the ghost her yearly offerings of rice and tea lay awake in his soft bed. He had dreamed that he was a prince, and a strange beast had asked him a riddle. Tomorrow, he would go and see the dream-interpreters.

The boy studied the pattern of the roof-wood. He is quiet, so as not to disturb his father and sisters with his fanciful dreams, which, after all, mean nothing. His father always told him that dreams were the province of the poor and the mad.

Outside his window, a squirrel left small footprints in the snow.

LICHEE GRASS WITHERS

In Kyoto, a scholar had fallen asleep in the midst of his scrolls, with his spectacles pushed up over his brows. In the cold morning, crows drew their wings close. Sleeping trees stood like soldiers at the gate.

Through an open window, a handsome brown moth fluttered into the room, landed lightly on the smooth hair of the sleeping scholar. It paused, as if in thought, flapping his wings with deliberate grace. It seemed to consider something brought on the snow-scented wind.

When the scholar's brow furrowed, deep in dreams, the moth lifted away from him, and out into the gray dawn.

EARTHWORMS TWIST
INTO KNOTS

At the foot of the dream-pagoda, the great red *torii* gate bent low to the ground and cracked under the weight of snow. Her scarlet paint shone horribly bright against the pale earth, as though blood had been spilled. She lay there like a great heart burst open, and the sound of her falling broke the genteel silence for only a moment.

The splintered posts which still stood straight later wounded slightly the foot of a late-migrating magpie.

She would be buried under the ice until the spring, when the cicadas would come to mate in her shadow.

THE ELK'S HORN BREAKS

On Mountain's east flank, a shaggy goat with massive horns chewed the tough winter grass. Snow caught in his fur in long matted strands. He balanced on the rocks, searching for the sweet moss he liked best in the winter months. It was difficult work, pebbles slipped into his hooves and down the cliffside, rattling like a shaman's staff.

As the clouds drifted over his back, he looked down towards the little valley, and thought briefly of the girl who could not climb her tower, how he pitied her, and how her hair smelled of cinnamon.

UNDERGROUND
SPRINGS MOVE

River refused to think on it.

Slabs of ice moved lazily down his current, grinding against each other as though they were carriages in the city. The fish dreamed and the trees bent low over the rippling stream, a thatched canopy.

If it was true that she could not step in him twice, then she had not stepped in *this* River at all, he reasoned. Perhaps, then, he had never known her, and therefore should not weep.

WILD GEESE RETURN TO THEIR NORTHERN HOME

The silkworm colony of the village suddenly ceased to produce their fine white thread. From the morning of Ayako's last dream on the Mountain, the generation which were then thriving in the house of the silk weavers produced nothing but a thick, viscous black fluid, which did not dry properly, leaving a strange, knotted coil. For seven worm-generations after this there was no good silk in the village, only the black cocoon-stuff. In the dreams of children the silkworms sang as they birthed it, and whispered that they were weaving a shroud for the death-festival of a ghost.

The boy saw this and was troubled. For no reason he thought of his beast-dream, and wondered what riddle would have this scythe-silk as its answer.

The villagers burned the dream-thread in the spring, and the smell of it lingered into midsummer, clinging to the temple bell-ropes and the granary doors.

MAGPIES NEST

The bones of Ayako still dreamed, but her lips had flushed blue and her body was cold. She had dreamed herself out of her shell, and it remained like a pale gem, slowly becoming dust on the highest floor of the dream-pagoda. She/I/we had composed our song, and moved away from the cocoon-tower to open our throats in the mountains. We left the meadow of shells-within-shells, where we lived within the body which lived within the pagoda which lived within the Mountain.

Perhaps one day there will be tower-shells and Mountain-shells glittering, too, on the grass.

We are finished. Our smile is beatific and mouthless. We have no more body to puzzle us, and our voices multiply in infinite combinations, through the trees and stones and snow:

When one possible woman dies, it is as though a shutter closes, and the light from a certain window is snuffed out. There are many more windows, and really, since the window had already been opened and shut an infinite number of times, since in potential it occupies both the states of Open and Shut, nothing changes at all. This process is indefinite, and cannot be charted.

THE PHEASANT CALLS
TO ITS MATE

The dream-bones of Ayako were not found until the next summer, when the boy whose lot it was to bring the ghost her offerings could not find her. He had not lost the lottery this year, but had traded a bowl of rice and three jade beads to the girl who had, so that he could see the old woman again, and ask her about his dreams.

When he climbed the pagoda and discovered her small heap of pearl-white bones, he was overcome, and wept for the woman who had told him about the dream of the Mountain. He could not decide what would be the correct thing to do with her bones—for it was now clear she had not actually been a ghost, even if she had since become one. So he gathered them up and placed them with some incense and the sack of rice in one of Mountain's secret clefts.

Until he was forty, and appointed, through his father's influence, to the royal court at Kyoto, the boy brought incense and rice to her bones at the death of each summer, faithful as a wife.

He would dream of her often, even in his city apartments hung with curtains he had ordered made from the black silk thread of that terrible year. And in his dreams she was young, a child, hiding under a wheelbarrow. She peered out, whispered to him that the fire-goddess had fallen in love with the village.

The dream interpreters would not speak with him.

CHICKENS BROOD

The I-that-is-Ayako tells you these things. It is my lesson, and I have told it. River heard, and Fox. Gate and Juniper listened, and Moth heard rumor of it.

The you-that-is-Ayako has heard it, too.

THE EAGLEHAWK FLIES FURIOUSLY HIGH

There was a storm the day the boy interred my bones within Mountain. The rain curled down to him in spirals, and the air crackled with the potential of lightning. The stones could hear the song my bones sang, the slight, susurring song of the discarded body. I felt them press in to hear, and the juniper trees bent to catch it.

THE WATERS AND SWAMPS
ARE THICK AND HARD

Alone, with the mist creeping in like a pale-mouthed thief,
Mountain wept.

.